THE FLIGHT
OF A FALLEN IDOL

As he whirled the horse about, he saw the two young Cheyennes converge their horses a little, making for the gap between the trees through which the fugitives had ridden, and now Torridon could see the grins of unearthly joy on their faces, the wild glitter of their eyes. Already they were tasting the pleasure of the coup, the death stroke, the scalping . . .

He raised his pistol. Both shots must bring down a man, for otherwise it would mean sudden death.

They saw that movement. One of them raised his lance and hurled it, but his horse at that moment stumbled, and though the range was short, the long, slender weapon went past Torridon's head with a soft, wavering hum which he would never forget to his death's day . . .

FUGITIVES' FIRE

BERKLEY BOOKS, NEW YORK

Fugitives' Fire was previously published in
two parts in *Western Story Magazine* in 1928
under the titles *Prairie Pawn* and *Fugitives' Fire*,
written under the pseudonym of Peter Henry Morland.

FUGITIVES' FIRE

A Berkley Book / published by arrangement with
G. P. Putnam's Sons

PRINTING HISTORY
Berkley edition / February 1991
Published simultaneously in hardcover by G. P. Putnam's Sons.

ISBN: 0-425-12559-9

A BERKLEY BOOK ® 757,375
Berkley Books are published by The Berkley Publishing Group,
200 Madison Avenue, New York, New York 10016.
The name "BERKLEY" and the "B" logo
are trademarks belonging to Berkley Publishing Corporation.

PRINTED IN THE UNITED STATES OF AMERICA

10 9 8 7 6 5 4 3 2 1

PART ONE

★

Prairie Pawn

CHAPTER I

★

Sad Music

In great good-humor was High Wolf and with reason. No fewer than twenty of his young men were on the warpath under the leadership of the young chiefs, Rising Hawk and Standing Bull, but still the man power of his camp was so great that he had been able to send out young and old to a great hunt, and a vastly successful one, so that now the whole camp was red with hanging buffalo meat and white with the great strips of back fat. It was not strange that the old warrior chose to wrap himself in his robe and walk slowly through the camp. Everywhere the women were at work, for now that the meat had been hung to dry, there was the labor of fleshing the many hides—cowhides for robes and lodge skins, bull hides for parfleche, shields, and everything that needed stiff and powerful leather. Three days like this, in a year's hunting, would keep the entire camp in affluence.

So, therefore, smiles and flashing teeth turned toward the chief as he went on his solitary way through the crowd, apparently oblivious of everything, but with his old eyes missing not the least of details, until he had completed the round of the tepees and returned to the center of the camp where, near his own big lodge there stood a still more brilliant tepee, a nineteen-skin beauty, of snowy hide, with just enough gaudy paint to show off its white texture.

Without envy, but with a critical eye, he regarded this lodge, moving from one side to another, as though anxious to make sure that all was well with it. Then he struck with his walking staff at the flap of the tent. He was asked to enter, and stepping inside, he

3

found there an old woman, busily beading moccasins. She rose to greet him. It was one of his own squaws, Young Willow, though there was nothing young about her except her name. Time had shrunk and bowed her a little, but her arms were still long and powerful, and she was known through the whole tribe for the work of her strong hands.

High Wolf tapped the hard floor of the lodge impatiently with his staff.

"Why are you not fleshing hides?" he asked. "It is not always summer. When winter comes, White Thunder will have to sit close to the fire, and even then his back will be cold. He will not have anything to wrap himself in."

In spite of the awe in which she held her husband and master, Young Willow allowed herself the luxury of a faint smile, and she waved to the furnishings of the tent. There was only one bed, but there were six back rests made of the slenderest willow shoots, strung on sinew, and covered with the softest robes; and between the back rests were great sacks of dried meat, corn, fruit. There were huge, square bundles, too, incased in dry rawhide, almost as stiff and strong as wood. One of these she opened. It was filled with folded robes and, lifting the uppermost one she displayed to her husband the inner surface, elaborately painted.

"And there are many more," said Young Willow. "There are so many more than he can use that I have to keep them in these bundles. He has enough to wear, enough to wrap his friends in in cold weather, enough to give away to the poor and the old warriors, and besides there are plenty to use for trade. He is rich, and there is no one else among the Cheyennes who is as rich as he! Look!"

She took up a bag and, jerking open its mouth, she allowed the chief to look down into a great mass of beads of all colors, all sizes. There were crystal beads that flashed like diamonds, there were beads of crimson, purple, yellow, black, gold, and brown. There were big and small beads, dull and bright beads.

Even the calm of the chief was broken a little and he grunted: "This is well! This is well! Who gave him all these beads?"

"Whistling Elk brought them yesterday," said the squaw.

"When he came in from the traders, you know that he brought many things. But most of his robes he had traded for these beads and he came to the tepee here and told White Thunder that he wanted him to have the beads. White Thunder did not want to take them."

The chief grunted.

"Why not?" he asked sharply. "Does a treasure like this fall down every day like dew on the ground?"

"White Thunder said that he had more than he required. But Whistling Elk reminded him that his son would have died, if White Thunder had not cured him with a strong medicine."

"I remember," said the old man. "That is very true. The son of Whistling Elk became very sick."

"He was as hot as fire," said the squaw. "The medicine men could not help him. Then White Thunder had him carried to this lodge. Listen to me! For three days he gave that boy nothing to eat except water in which meat had been boiled. He wrapped him in cold clothes, too. On the fourth day the boy began to sweat terribly. His mother was sitting beside him and she began to cry and mourn. She said that her son was melting away. But White Thunder smiled. He said that the sickness was melting away and not the body. He was right. The boy slept, and when he opened his eyes, they were clear and bright. In half a moon he could walk with the other boys."

"I remember it." The chief nodded. "Heammawihio has clothed White Thunder with power as he clothes a tree with green leaves. If he is rich now, still he is not rich enough."

"He has sixty horses in the herd," said the woman.

"Still he is not rich enough," said High Wolf. "I have given you to this tepee to take care of him and cook for him. It would be better for you to displease me than to displease him. It would be better for you to displease under-water spirits than to displease him, Young Willow!"

He spoke so sternly that she shrank from him a little, and immediately explained: "Wind Woman and three young girls are all working to flesh hides for White Thunder. They can do more than I can do alone. Besides, I am working here at this beading to make him happy."

She showed the moccasin and the chief deigned to examine it with some care. He handed it back with a grunt and a nod.

"He did not go to the hunt," said he. "Why did he not go? Was he sick?"

"His heart is sick, not his body," said the squaw sullenly. "He has all that any warrior could want, and yet he is not a warrior. Look! There is always meat steaming in the pot! It is the best meat. There is always fat in it. The flesh of old bulls is never given to him. The dried meat of young, tender cows and calves fills those sacks. He lives like a great chief. But he is not a chief. He has never made a scalp shirt. He has never taken a scalp or killed an enemy or counted a coup!"

"So!" said the chief. "You work for him with your hands, but in your heart you despise him!"

She answered sullenly: "Why should I not? He is not like us! There is no young man in the camp who is not stronger and taller!"

The chief made a little pause in which his anger seemed to rise.

"What young man," he said, "has come to us from among the Sky People?"

She was silent, shrugging her shoulders.

"What young man," said he, "could drive off the water spirits when they were tearing down the banks of a great river?"

At this she blinked a little. as though remembering something important, but half forgotten.

"What young man among us, or what old man, either, what great doctor or medicine man," went on High Wolf with rising sternness, "was able to bring the rain? The corn withered. Dust covered the prairie. In the winter we should have starved. But White Thunder went out and called once, and immediately the clouds jumped up in the south. He called again and the clouds covered the sky. The third time he cried out, the rain washed our faces and ran down to the roots of the dying corn; but these things you forget!"

"No," she muttered, "I never shall forget that day. No Cheyenne ever has seen such strong medicine working."

"But you," went on the chief sternly, "are not contented with such things. What are scalps and scalp-takers compared to the strength of a man who can call down the Sky People to help him? Since Standing Bull brought him to us, everything we do is lucky. There is no drought. The young men and the children do not die of sickness. The buffalo come up and stand at the edge of our camp and wait for us to surround and shoot them down. Our war parties have struck the Crows and the Pawnee wolves and brought back horses and scalps, and counted many coups. But this man is not great enough for you to serve! You despise him in your heart while you work with your hands. Do you think that he does not know? I tell you, Young Willow, that he sees the thoughts in your heart as clearly as he sees the paintings on his tepee!"

This speech he delivered in a stern and gloomy voice, and the squaw began to bite her lips nervously.

"I am willing to work for him," she whined. "All day my hands never stop."

"There are other women who would work for him," said the chief. "There are other women who would be glad to live in the presence of such good medicine all day long."

"All day he never speaks," she answered in feeble self-defense. "There are many back rests in this lodge. It is a lodge for a great and noble chief to fill with feasting and friends. But he never calls in friends, except Standing Bull or Rising Hawk. He would rather sit on his bed of rye grass and rushes, wrapped in an unpainted robe. Then he takes a flute of juniper wood and makes sad music, like a young man in love. Or he goes down to the river and sits on the banks. The three young warriors who have to be with him to guard him, they stand and yawn and wish to be hunting or on the warpath, but he sits and plays the flute. Or else he takes his pistol from his breast and shoots little birds that fly overhead near him. Even a child would be ashamed of such a life!"

"Can a child take a pistol and shoot little birds out of the air?" asked the chief sharply. "Can any of the warriors do that?"

"No man could do it," she replied. "It is medicine that kills them with the flash of his pistol. But when does he take the war rifle and go on the warpath?"

"You speak," said the chief slowly, "like a fool and the daughter of a fool. But you have given me a thought. If he makes sad music on the flute, it is because he has seen some beautiful girl among the Cheyennes. He is in love. Now, Young Willow, learn the name of the girl he has seen, and he shall have her, and you—you shall come into my lodge and name the thing you want as a reward. Only learn the name of the girl he wants!"

CHAPTER II

★

A Wonder Horse

Under a spreading willow on the bank of the river lay White Thunder, his hands beneath his head, his sad eyes looking up through the thin branches, noting how they changed their pattern against the sky as the wind stirred them. He looked neither to the right nor to the left, because in so doing, he would be forced to see the three who guarded him. Every moon three chosen and proved young warriors were told off to watch him day and night. In the day they never left his side except when he entered his tepee. And in the night they slept or watched outside his lodge. The vigilance of the Cheyennes netted Paul Torridon about in the dark and in the daylight, so that he had given up all hope of escape from them. If there were any hope left to him, it was something which he could not visualize, something which would scatter the tribe and by a merciful accident leave him free to return to his kind. Particularly he wished to avoid the attention of these three, because he knew their hearts were burning with anger against him. They had yearned to go off with the hunt but, since he refused, they were forced to remain idly in camp watching him instead of flying their horses among the wild buffalo—a sport for a king!

The three were talking, softly. For though they despised him, they held him in awe, also. As a man, he was to them less than nothing. As a communer with the spirits, he was a dreadful power. Now they mentioned a familiar name. Torridon half closed his eyes.

"What do you say of my horse?" he asked.

"I say," answered a voice, "that the horse would come to you even through a running river."

Another answered sharply: "And I say that no horse will swim unless it is forced. It would be a strong medicine, for instance, that would make a horse go into that stream! A horse has no hands to push himself away from sharp rocks!"

Torridon thrust himself up on one arm, and shook back the hair from his face. It was quite true that the river beneath them was not a pleasant ford for horses. Men could manage it easily enough, but it was thickly strewn with rocks, and among the rocks the current drove down strongly.

Torridon whistled, and up to him came a black stallion at a sharp trot, and standing before him, actually lowered his fine head and sniffed at the hand of his master as though to inquire his meaning.

The three young braves looked on with hearts that swelled with awe.

"Do you fear the water, Ashur?" asked Torridon in Cheyenne.

He flung out his hand in a little gesture, and that gesture made the horse turn his head toward the river. But so seemingly did Ashur understand the question, so human was that turning of the head to look at the water that the young braves murmured softly to one another.

"You see," said Torridon, who was not above a little charlatanry from time to time, "that he has no fear of the water. He asks me for what purpose he should go into it, however."

The young Cheyennes were filled with amazement.

"But in what manner did he speak?" asked the eldest, who had taken his scalp in regular battle and therefore was the accepted leader of the little party. "For I did not hear a sound."

"Tell me," said the untruthful Torridon, "do you have a sign language?"

"Yes, with which every Indian can speak."

"Well, then, a horse has signs, also."

"But a horse has no fingers with which to make signs."

"He has a tail, however," said Torridon smoothly, "and also two ears, and a head to nod or shake, and four hoofs to stamp."

There was a general exclamation of wonder.

"However," said the scalp taker a little sullenly, "I still think that no horse would cross that water, except under a whip."

Torridon pretended to frown.

"Do you think," said he, "that when I put a spell on a horse it is less than a whip on his back?"

"Even a child," replied the young warrior truthfully, "may speak about great things."

"Very well," said Torridon, "this is a knife which you have admired."

He took from his belt a really beautiful weapon, the point curving only slightly from the straight, the steel of the finest quality, with the glimmer of a summer blue sky close to the sun. The haft was ornamented with inset beadwork, to roughen the grip. It was a treasure which Torridon had received from a grateful brave to whom he had given good fortune on the warpath, the fortune immediately being proved by the counting of a coup and the capture of five good horses!

"It is true," said the young Cheyenne, his eyes blazing in his head. "But," he added, "what have I to offer against it?"

"You have a new rifle," said Torridon carelessly.

The other sighed. The rifle was a very good one. It was the pride of his young life. However, the knife was a gaudy trinket which inflamed his very heart with lust to own it, and he reassured himself by looking down at the dangerous water.

Besides, a horse was to be persuaded through the midst of that water without the use of a whip or a spur, and with no man on its back to direct it. He nodded as he turned again to Torridon.

"Look!" he exclaimed suddenly. And he laid the rifle at the feet of a companion.

"And there is the knife," said Torridon.

He took it again from his belt and, with a little flick of the wrist which he had learned from Rising Hawk, he drove it half the length of its blade into the ground before their companion.

Then he rose to attempt the venture. On the edge of the bank he took off his clothes. White as polished marble he flashed beneath that strong sun. The wind blew his hair aside, and he laughed with pleasure at the cool touch of the air and the angry hand of the sun.

The Indians looked significantly at one another, partly admiring and partly in contempt. The Cheyennes were huge specimens of manhood. He was of small account who stood under six feet in height, and they had shoulders and limbs to match; but Torridon was made slenderly, tapering and graceful. He was fast of foot, the Indian youth knew. How would he appear in the water?

He did not leave them long in doubt. He merely paused to adjust a head band that would bind his unbarbered hair. Then he dived from the bank.

There was only a slight sound as he took the water. Then, through the black shadow of the pool under the bank, they saw him rise glimmering. He struck out through the current. It was true that he had not the might of arm that many of them possessed. But neither did he have their bulk to drag through the water, and he used the stroke which Roger Lincoln, that flawless hero of the plain, had taught him.

"It's only in the brain that you can beat an Indian," Roger Lincoln had been fond of saying. And he had taught Torridon many things as they voyaged over the plains together. A most unreceptive mind had dreamy Paul Torridon for woodcraft or for the arts of hunting, but at least he could learn the craft of swimming from a perfect master.

He glided rapidly through the water, now, lying face down, rolling a little from side to side to breathe, and the long strokes of the arms and the thrashing feet carried him rapidly through the stream.

He could hear them on the bank behind him calling: "Hai! He is being pulled by a string!"

He swerved past a reaching rock, stepped on another, and leaped onto the farther bank. There he wrung the water from his long hair and waved a flashing arm.

"Ashur!" he called.

The black stallion was already at the brink of the stream, looking wistfully after his master. At this call, he advanced his forefeet into the water and sniffed at it, but immediately he withdrew and bounded away, throwing his heels into the air.

The wagerer shouted with triumph: "The knife is mine, White Thunder."

Torridon made no reply. He sat down dripping on the bank, and seemed more interested in the flight of a hawk which was swinging lower and lower through the sky above them.

"Come back, White Thunder!" cried the brave. "You see he never will take the water!"

Now for answer Torridon raised an arm and pointed. He was more than half ashamed of himself to resort to such trickery and sham. But, after all, these people had forced the rôle of medicine man upon him quite against his will. They had dressed him up in fake garments of mystery, they had stolen him away from the girl he loved and from his best of friends. It was hardly more than fair that they should be called upon to take something for which they were even asking. So he pointed at the descending hawk, as though it were a symbol sent down to him from the Sky People, who were so eternally on the tongues of the Cheyennes.

It made a great sensation among the three braves. Torridon saw them pointing, and whispering together, and he with whom Torridon had made the wager hastily caught up a handful of pebbles and sand and began to shift them from hand to hand, blowing strongly on them—making medicine against the medicine maker!

Torridon laughed. They would take that laughter for invincible scorn of them. As a matter of fact, it was pure amusement and good nature. Of Ashur he had had no doubt from the first.

Now indeed the black horse returned to the edge of the water. He sent one whinney of complaint across to his master, and straightway he plunged in. Torridon was very confident. Out here on the plains the rivers were few and far between. They were apt to be comparatively still, also. But where Ashur was raised, two stormy creeks had cut the grazing lands, and the horse which aspired to the richer, farther pastures had to cross them both. From colthood Ashur had been a master of the difficult craft.

He came swiftly, snorting the froth and water from his nostrils, so low did he carry his head, stretching it forth over the surface. A smooth, strong glide of water seized him and dropped him through a narrow passage between reaching rocks. That instant the heart of Torridon stood still and he regretted the bet. But now Ashur came again, more strongly than ever, pricking his little ears in recognition of the master who waited for him. A moment more and his forefeet grounded. He climbed out, shook himself, and then leaping to the side of Torridon, he turned and cast back at the young warriors a ringing neigh of almost human defiance.

CHAPTER III

★

Young Willow's Malice

A shout of mingled wonder and applause came across the water to Torridon, but he had turned his head toward the plains which stretched off to the north. Naked as he was, weaponless, for an instant he was on the verge of throwing himself on the back of Ashur and flying away into the wilderness. But when he looked back to the farther shore, he saw that three rifles were gripped in three ready pairs of hands. It was their business to watch him, and watch him they would—aye, and scalp him gladly if the worst came to the worst!

He abandoned his thought with a sigh and then swam back to the waiting three. Ashur followed him obediently, his nose in the little smother of water raised by the kicking heels of his master. The rocks reached for the fine horse again, and in vain, and Torridon stood again with his guards, whipping the water from his body with the edge of his hand, laughing and panting.

"Look!" cried the youngest of the three warriors suddenly, but in a voice muffled with awe. "He has brought down the power from the clouds, and now he is going back again!"

He pointed, and Torridon, turning his head, saw that the hawk was rising even more swiftly than it had descended. He laughed again to himself. No doubt, this tale, liberally reënforced by the imaginations of the three, would soon be circling the village and adding to the great stock of folly and lies which already circulated about him among the Cheyennes.

The eldest of the trio took up his rifle and laid it at Torridon's feet.

"When I made the bet," he said, "I forgot that you could command the air spirits out of their places. Of course they made the horse light and showed him where to swim through the rocks!"

"I saw a ripple go before him," said the youngest of the three gravely. "Of course something invisible was stopping the current to let the horse through! This is a great wonder. I, who did not see the making of the rain, at last have seen this!"

Torridon dressed quickly. There was not much dressing to do, for he was equipped like any other young Cheyenne in breech clout, leggings, and a shirt. There were distinctions, for the leather was the softest of deerskin, white as snow, and worked over in delicate designs with beads and porcupine quills, while the outer fringe of the leggings was enriched with glittering beads and even some spurious hoofs of buffalo, polished highly. He put on his moccasins first, and stepped into the rest of his apparel, after wriggling into the tightly fitted shirt. Then he sat down and began to dry his hair, by spreading it to the sun and the wind.

The three regarded him with profoundest silence. They had seen such things that it was well to be quiet for a time, and rehearse the affairs to their own minds. Afterward, even the elders would be glad to invite them to feasts and let them talk of the prodigies which White Thunder on this day had performed. One of them had turned the hawk into an eagle, already, in his mind's eye. And another had made out the form of the water spirit which drew the stallion through the river.

At last, Torridon took up the rifle which was his prize. He examined it with care.

"Rushing Wind," said he to the young man who had given up the gun, "how many times have you fired this?"

"Three times."

"And what did it do?"

"It killed three buffalo," said Rushing Wind, his breast heaving just once with mingled pride in the weapon and grief because of its loss.

Torridon handed it back to its first owner.

"Take it again," said he. "It is good medicine in your hands. I already have many guns in my lodge. I do not want to empty yours. Besides," he added shamelessly, "as you have seen, I have other things than guns with which to do what I wish!"

The latter part of this speech was accepted by the young men with nodding heads. But Rushing Wind hesitated about the return.

"My brother is rich," said he; "nevertheless, even a rich man wants something with which to remember a great day."

"That is true," agreed Torridon.

He reached out and took the knife from the belt of Rushing Wind. He replaced it with his own rich knife and waved his hand.

"By that exchange," said he, "we can remember one another!"

Rushing Wind returned no answer. He had seen himself, a moment before, compelled to fall back upon the war bow and arrow. Now, not only was the rifle his once more but, in addition, he wore at his belt such a jewel as would make even the great war chiefs look on him with envious eyes. His heart was too full for utterance, so that he was forced to scowl bitterly.

Torridon, understanding perfectly, arose to cover the confusion of the warrior and led the way back to the camp. At the door of the lodge he invited them to enter; they as perfunctorily refused, to remain lounging outside, while he entered the cool shadow of the tepee. He was still amused, still inclined to laugh to himself so that Young Willow, at her beading, glanced keenly at him.

She was a little afraid of this youth, though as the daughter of one great war chief and the wife of another, she despised this counter of no coups, this taker of no scalps. He was an outlander. The joys and the sorrows of the tribe did not affect him, he pretended no interest. Their victories were things at which he shrugged his shoulders; their dances and celebrations left him cold and unstirred. Therefore, she both hated and despised him, but also she was afraid. She, with her own eyes, while all the tribe was witness, had seen him call up the rain clouds. At his bidding, the lightning had flashed and the thunder had roared. He had disappeared in the middle of the confusion. Some said that he simply had ridden off through the darkness of the storm, but it was whispered everywhere that no mortal could have ridden through the assembled Cheyennes at that time. Had he not been wrapped in a storm cloud and snatched away?

For her own part, she knew that she was honored to have been selected as the keeper of this lodge; and as such, all that she said was now listened to, and the chief men of the nation stopped her when she was abroad and asked after the latest doing of White Thunder. If there were little to tell of interest, fortunately Young Willow had a sufficient imagination; no audience that asked wonders of her should go away with empty ears!

Now the youth sat smiling to himself.

"White Thunder," said she, "where is the knife that you wore at your belt?"

"I have given it to Rushing Wind."

She raised her head.

"Do you know that that is a medicine knife, worth five horses if it is worth a handful of dried meat?"

"So I was told."

She muttered angrily: "One spendthrift makes a naked lodge. You gave away the white saddle yesterday?"

"The young man had nothing but a buffalo robe to ride on."

"It is not the seat that makes the horseman," said this quoter of proverbs, "neither is the horse judged by the saddle!"

"Saddle and mane make a horse sell," retorted he, having picked up some of the same sort of language from this ancient gossip.

Fairly stopped by this, she returned to her beading. It was true that the goods in this tepee were not hers, and it was also true that the generosity of the Cheyennes was flooding the lodge constantly with more than the master of it could use. Nevertheless, she was old enough to be parsimonious. The aged ask for a full house and larder.

Torridon lounged against a supple back rest and raised his eyes to the top of the tepee with a great sigh. Time, time, time! How slowly it went!

"Aye," said Young Willow, spiteful after her last silencing, "You may well sigh! For in a hundred winters we shall all be bald!"

"That is true," he answered, "and it is also true that even a little time will hatch a great mischief."

She looked askance at him, rather suspecting that there was a
sting in this speech, but not quite confident of the point. So she
pursed her withered lips and consulted her profound heart to find
something more to say.

He, in the meantime, began to finger some of the articles which
hung beside the back rest, taking down a great war bow of the
horn of mountain sheep, tough and elastic, able to send an arrow
four hundred yards in battle, or, in the hunt, drive a shaft to the
three feathers into the tough side of a buffalo bull.

"A strong bow for a strong hand; for the weak hand it is a
walking staff," said the venomous old woman.

"Yes," said Torridon, "or it would do as a whip."

She caught her breath and mumbled, but the reply was too apt
not to silence her again.

He laid aside the bow and picked up the favorite solace of his
quiet hours. It was a flute of the juniper wood, from which one
could draw plaintive sounds, and by much practice upon it, he was
able to perform with a good deal of skill.

He tried it now, very softly. And he half closed his eyes in sad
enjoyment of the harmony he made, for the sorrowful love sorrow.

As for Young Willow, she would have admitted at another time
that it was excellent music, and she would to-morrow attribute the
skill of the youth with the instrument to the direct intervention and
assistance of the Sky People. Now, however, she was looking for
trouble.

"Sorrow, sorrow, sorrow!" she muttered. "A sorrowing child is
never fat!"

He lowered the flute from his lips and looked vaguely upon her,
as though he had only half heard what she said.

So she, glad of a quiet audience, went on sharply: "And sorrow
and love are brother and sister. They go hand in hand. Who is the
girl that you make music for, White Thunder?"

At this, he actually dropped the flute and sat bolt upright,
staring at her, and very wide awake indeed.

Young Willow pretended to go on with her beading, but her grin
was very broad, so that it exposed her toothless, dark gums. She
had stung him at last.

CHAPTER IV

──────── ★ ────────

Disaster

Said Young Willow, busy at her work, or apparently busy: "There are many beautiful maidens among the Cheyennes. Even the Sky People draw down from the clouds, and wonder at them."

"That is true," agreed he, absently.

He had been too amazed by her remark to pay much heed to what followed.

"So," said Young Willow, "it is no wonder that you, White Thunder, should have come down to us. Tell me, therefore, the name of the girl."

"Of what use would it be if I should tell you?" said he.

"Of what use? I would myself go to High Wolf, and he would go to the father of the girl. Presently all would be arranged with the father."

"And she would be brought home to this lodge?"

"Yes."

Torridon smiled faintly, and the squaw frowned, unable to read his mind, no matter how hard she tried. She was angry with herself, when she found that she was baffled so early and so often by this youth. His white skin was a barrier that stopped her probing eyes, as it were.

"What should I do with a woman?" said Torridon.

"A wife is better than many horses," said the squaw sententiously. Torridon fell amiably into that mode of maintaining the discourse. In a way, he feared to be left to his own thoughts, for since Young Willow had turned the conversation into this channel the picture of Nancy Brett stood like life before him, in all her beauty, her gentleness, her grace. He tried to turn from that hopeless dream into the present. So he answered the squaw: "A bag of fleas is easier to keep watch over than a woman."

"Ha?" cried the squaw. "I think you are talking about the Arapahoes, or the Dakotas. You do not know our Cheyenne girls. After the sun has gone down, they still have firelight to work by."

"People who work forever," quoted Torridon, "are dull companions. You cannot dig up wisdom like a root."

Young Willow grunted. Her eyes had a touch of red fire in them as she glared across the tepee at her young companion.

"You cannot judge a woman by her tongue," she replied.

"No," said Torridon, "but with a small tongue, a woman can kill a tall man."

"Very well," grumbled Young Willow, "but you know the saying: A woman's council may be no great thing, but he is a fool who does not take it. I am giving you good advice, White Thunder."

"No doubt you are," yawned Torridon rather impolitely.

"Aye," she answered, "but only a pretty woman is always right."

"No," he replied, "a pretty woman is either silly or proud."

"For a proud woman," said she, "take a heavy hand."

He raised his slender hand with a sigh.

"My hand is not heavy, Young Willow. Even if I had a lovely wife, how could I keep her?"

"With a whip, perhaps."

"A Cheyenne girl," said he, more seriously, "wants a strong husband. She wants to see scalps drying in the lodge and hear her man counting his coups."

"You are young," said Young Willow tactfully, for she had been pleased to the core of her heart by the remark dispraising beauty in woman. "You are young, and a man is not grown in a summer."

"I never shall take scalps," said Torridon, sighing again. "I never shall count coups, or steal horses. How could I be honored among the Cheyennes or by a woman in my own lodge?"

This plain statement of fact took Young Willow a good deal

aback. It was, in short, what she had said at greater length to High Wolf. But at last she replied: "Take a wife, and I shall teach her how to behave. She will not be able to draw a breath that I shall not count. Afterward, you will have sons. You will be a great chief."

She painted the rosy picture with a good deal of warmth. And suddenly Torridon said gravely: "Let us talk no more about it, Young Willow. Are you tired of doing the work in this lodge?"

"I? No, no!" cried the squaw.

"Then stay with me, and I shall not ask for a Cheyenne girl as a wife. There is only one woman in the world whom I could marry, Young Willow."

"And she is not in this camp?"

"She is far away."

"She is a Blackfoot," said Young Willow instantly. "They are tall, and a short man wants a tall wife. They have big eyes, and the white men love only big eyes."

Her own small eyes became mere glints of light.

"No," said Torridon. "Big eyes are good to look at, but not to look. It is not a Blackfoot girl. I never have seen a Blackfoot."

"Then you have seen a Sioux girl smiling. They always are smiling, and they always are untrue."

"In short," said Torridon impatiently, "it is no Indian girl at all."

"A white woman?" asked Young Willow.

"Yes."

"She is tall and proud and rich," said Young Willow.

"No, she is small," mused Torridon. "Or rather, she is no size at all, but she fits into my mind and heart—"

"As the saddle fits the back of a horse," suggested Young Willow.

Torridon merely sighed.

"When you were carried away in the storm," said the squaw, "and disappeared over the prairie, then you went to Fort Kendry to find her there?"

But, at this direct question, Torridon recovered from his dream, and shrugged his shoulders.

"I am going to sleep," he said abruptly.

He settled back against the rest and closed his eyes. Young Willow was too well trained in the lodge of her husband to utter a word when one of the lords of creation was resting. Therefore, Torridon heard nothing except the light, faint click of beads in the rapid fingers of the squaw from time to time.

And he passed into another of the weary, sad vigils which he had kept so many times before. At last he actually slept and dreamed of great woe and misery: a dream so vivid that dreary, wailing voices thrummed in his ears loudly—and he wakened to find that the sounds were no dream at all, but that from hundreds of throats, apparently, a pæan of grief was rising through the village. The noise came slowly toward the tepee. He heard the screaming of women, who seemed maddened with woe.

Young Willow dashed into the lodge, her hair flying in long strings, her breast heaving.

"Why do so many people cry out, Young Willow?" he asked her, bewildered.

"You!" shrieked the squaw, shaking her bony fist at him. "You that make medicine when you wish, but let our men go out to die! It would have been better for us if you had been left in the sky!"

"But what has happened? Has some one died?"

"Has some one died?" exclaimed the squaw. "Eleven men are dead and Rising Hawk has brought home the rest, and all of the eight are wounded."

"Rising Hawk has brought them home?" exclaimed Torridon. "Then tell me what has become of Standing Bull?"

"He was lost! He was lost! He was captured in the battle and carried away by the Dakotas, and by this time they are eating his heart! He was your friend! He was your friend! Could you make no medicine for him?"

She ran out of the lodge again, raising her voice in a shrill keen as she burst through the entrance.

Torridon, amazed and shocked, followed. It was to Standing Bull that he owed his first captivity in the tribe. It was to Standing Bull, also, that he owed his recapture after the first escape. And yet he had been so much with the Cheyenne giant that he was shocked to hear of his capture. There was little chance that such a warrior as Standing Bull would be spared except for the sake of tormenting him slowly to death when the Dakotas had reached their homes after the war raid.

Torridon wrapped himself hastily in a robe and stepped into the entrance of the tepee in time to see the mass of the crowd of mourners move past. Every relative of a dead or wounded man was called upon by invincible custom to mourn, and with a dozen deaths to account for, it seemed that half the tribe was officially interested.

At that moment, Owl Woman went by. She was the young squaw of Standing Bull, the mother of his son, and as handsome a woman as could be found in the tribe. She had disfigured herself for life. Her hair was shaved from her head, and the scalp gashed across and across, so that blood had poured down and blackened over her face and shoulders. She went with bare legs, and along the calves she had ripped up the flesh again. As a crowning token of her affliction, she had actually cut off a finger of her left hand, and what with loss of blood and the shock of her grief and the torment of her exhaustion, she staggered rather than walked, her head rolled on her shoulders, and Torridon could hear her sobbing. It was not the noise of weeping, but the heavy gasp of exhaustion and hysteria.

The other mourners made way for her, partly because no victim had been of so high a rank as her husband, and partly because she had honored herself and the whole nation by this perfect expression of her grief. A dreadful picture of despair and madness, she staggered on past Torridon and he closed his eyes, feeling very sick indeed at the sight.

He did not need to ask questions. From the babble of the crowd and the exclamations of the mourners he learned the details sufficiently. Standing Bull and Rising Hawk actually had pushed so far into the land of the Dakotas that they had entered the deep and narrow ravine leading toward the village over which Spotted Antelope was the great chief. But while they were passing through, that formidable warrior had fallen upon them, taken them in the rear with a mighty attack, and crushed them.

Standing Bull had indeed played the hero. He had allowed the remnant to get away, assisted as they were by the savage fighting of Rising Hawk, who indeed had actually found time to count four coups and take a scalp in the short encounter.

The sound of the mourning rolled farther away, though the very heart of Torridon still was stabbed from time to time by the sudden shriek of a woman. He opened his eyes, and saw before him the silent form of High Wolf, robed to the eyes, and those eyes were fixed on the face of Torridon with a terrible malignity.

CHAPTER V

★

A Hawk Hangs High

It was plain to Torridon that the anger of the war chief was less because of the loss which had fallen upon the young braves of his tribe than because of some passion which he held against the white man himself.

"How!" said Torridon in quiet greeting.

The chief, uninvited, strode past him to the interior of the lodge, and Torridon followed him, seeing that some tiding of grave importance was about to be communicated to him. When he faced High Wolf, the latter said harshly: "It is true that White Thunder does not love Standing Bull. Standing Bull brought him to the Cheyennes. On account of that, White Thunder has given over the whole war party to the Dakotas. Twelve men are dead! Twelve men are dead and scalped, or else they are in the hands of the enemy. Why have you done this thing, White Thunder? If you did not love Standing Bull—well, you have the thunders in your hand and you can throw the lightning. Why did you not kill him and let the rest go?"

The first impulse of Torridon was open and frank disavowal, but suddenly he saw that merely to protest was of no avail whatever. To these red children of the prairie, he was the possessor of the most wonderful and potent "medicine" and, if he wished, he could extend the ægis of his might over all their war parties, even the most distant. To deny that he possessed that power would, in the eyes of High Wolf, make him appear the merest hypocrite. It might mean, at once, a knife in the throat, or slow burning over a fire. He thought of this as he looked the old

26

chief in the eye and answered slowly: "Even good medicine may be used wrongly."

High Wolf blinked and then frowned.

"Then what did they do? Did you make medicine for them, after all? No man heard you so much as sing a song when they left the camp."

"Why should I sing songs or shake rattles like the other medicine men?" asked Torridon scornfully. "When the corn was dying and the dust was deep and white on the plains, did I sing a song to make the rain come?"

"You called to it," said High Wolf, "and the heavens were covered with clouds. Why did you not call again, and send strength to Standing Bull?"

"If they had gone slowly and laid in wait," said Torridon, on the spur of the moment, "they would have had no harm. But they ran in like wild buffalo, and like buffalo they were killed."

High Wolf apparently checked an angry exclamation. Then he replied: "Before the night comes, we send out fifty braves to go north. Tell me, White Thunder. What will be their fortune?"

Torridon was taken well aback. He had had to make "medicine" for these strange people before, but he had not been called upon to make prophecies.

As Torridon paused, the chief continued: "Now Spotted Antelope rides far south from his village. He waits for us. How shall we pass him, or how shall we fight against him? He has two or three score fighting men. Their hearts are big. They laugh at the Cheyennes! What medicine have you for that, White Thunder?"

Like one who has his back against the wall, Torridon replied: "What is the use in sending the Sky People to help the Cheyennes, when the Cheyennes will not know how to use them?"

The return of the chief fairly took his breath.

"You have been one who speaks with a single tongue in the camp of the Cheyennes. Tell me now, White Thunder: Will you give me your promise to ride with a war party against the Dakotas and never try to escape from them? Will you go with them, and make the Sky People fight on our side?"

There was no possibility of refusal. The passion of the chief swept Torridon before it, like a cork on a flood. He dared not resist.

"I can give you my word," he said gloomily.

High Wolf paused, his eyes still glittering.

"I go to the young men," he said. "Rising Hawk burns like a fire. He shall ride out again in spite of his wound. You, then, will ride with them and give them fortune?"

Torridon, dumb with amazement and woe, merely nodded, and the old man was gone, leaving the boy regarding earnestly a most terrible fate. He had but the slenderest doubt as to what would come of this. Pawnee or Crow or Blackfoot, all were dangerous enough, but the Dakotas, each as able a warrior as ever bestrode a horse, were distinguished above all for their swarming numbers. They could redden the plains with their men, if they so chose. He who invaded their country was like a fly walking into a spider's web!

Young Willow came back into the lodge and, in silence, set about cleaning the rifle, though it needed no cleaning, and then laying out a pack which consisted of dried meat and ammunition, together with a few other necessaries. Plainly, she had been told to do these things by High Wolf. And when Torridon glanced at her, he thought that he spied a settled malice in her expression.

Ashur was brought, the saddle put on him. Still the sounds of mourning filled the camp, but other noises were blended with them. Wild yells and whoops cut the air; somewhere a battle song was being chanted, and going to the entrance of the lodge, Torridon saw half a dozen braves in front of their tepees dancing about in the fantastic step of stiff-legged roosters. All were painted for war; several were wearing war bonnets of eagle feathers. Near by their horses were being prepared by industrious squaws, just as Ashur was being fitted.

The preparation was speedy. Torridon had known war parties to make medicine and go through formalities for a fortnight. Now everything was rushed through: the Cheyennes were red hot for vengeance and old customs had to give way before the pressure.

For his own part, he wondered that, on an expedition of such importance, every man worthy of carrying arms was not enlisted, leaving the defense of the camp to the very old and the very young. But Indian measures were rarely so whole-hearted as this. They loved war and they loved scalps, but they hated to commit all their forces to a single action. They believed in skirmishes rather than in pitched battles.

So at last Rising Hawk was seen, mounted on a spirited pony, a dressing on his left forearm, which had been cut across by a bullet in the late action. Before him went two medicine men, complete in masks and medicine bags, and all the weird implements of their profession. As they came closer, they halted and held back, and one who had a mask like a wolf's head over his shoulders, pointed at Torridon, and then turned away.

Of course they were jealous of him and of his reputation. Their income for healings and for soothsayings had fallen away sharply since the coming of the white man to their camp, with his marvels of rain making, and all the rest. No doubt, in their heart of hearts they were wishing the worst of ill fortune upon the expedition which he was to accompany.

Rising Hawk, however, greeted the white man courteously. Torridon mounted. They rode on from the camp. The warriors fell in behind them. Children and young braves rushed out to see them pass, and so the procession grew.

At the edge of the camp, they broke into a gallop. Young boys, yelling like demons, rushed bareback before and behind them, and whirled around them like leaves in a wind. And so they were escorted as far as the verge of the river. Up its bank they passed until they came to the ford, crossed this, and at last they were committed to the width of the prairies.

Torridon turned in the saddle, on the farther bank, and looked across the stream and back to the distant village. He felt almost a touch of homesickness in seeing it thus. Anything was preferable to that grim expedition against so dangerous a foe as the Sioux. But the die had been cast and he was committed. Even so, he could not help considering a sudden break away from the Cheyennes, and then trusting the speed of the black stallion to take him safely out of range of the pursuing bullets.

His honor held him, albeit by a single thread, and he remained trailing at the rear of the party, full of his thoughts.

A horseman dropped back beside him. It was Rushing Wind, his late guard, who was pointing an excited hand at the sky.

"Look, White Thunder, already your thoughts are answered by the Sky People. They have sent down their messenger to give you good fortune again!"

Torridon followed the direction of the pointing arm and saw that a hawk was circling slowly above them, keeping pace with the progress of the party. He forced back a melancholy smile from his lips.

But in the meantime, every brave in the party had already taken note of that hanging hawk against the sky, and the same thought seemed to fill every breast. Their eyes flashed. Rising Hawk could not keep from raising his long lance and shaking it victoriously against the sky, and the braves went onward with a great gayety of demeanor. Already they had forgotten the recent crushing defeat which the Sioux had inflicted upon their nation. They were as full of confidence as a body of children at play.

CHAPTER VI

★

On the Warpath

As though the sting of the wound in his arm was a constant spur, they went north like the wind, with Rising Hawk constantly urging them to greater efforts. A dozen horses dropped dead under the fierce riding. That was in the early days, and the rest grew thin, but wonderfully hard and fit, and the boys were easily able to keep the horse herd within striking distance of the riders. Torridon spared Ashur every other day. But even those alternate journeys on random ponies hardly were necessary, for Ashur was laughing at the miles. All his running under Torridon or with the herd barely had sufficed to thumb a little of the flesh off his ribs and cut the line of his belly a little harder and higher. But on the days when he ranged with the herd, the Indian boys were happy. There were four of them, like four young winged imps, ever flying here and there, merciless to the steeds, slaves to the braves on the warpath. But when Ashur ran with the herd, their work was nothing. He ranged back and forth at the rear of the trotting ponies. He guarded and guided them like sheep, and they feared him and respected him. He was a king among them.

His size, his grandeur, his lofty air and matchless speed made Torridon feel every day more keenly his own lack of force of hand. He was as no one in the party! Surely, in battle, the least of all the warriors would do far more than he.

In the day he was little regarded, but in the evening, after food, Rising Hawk and the chief men of the party were sure to draw close to him and discuss plans and futures. He was very reticent. He had been forced to promise them good fortune. If that good fortune did not develop he would get his throat cut as a reward for his false prophecy. In the meantime, he would not speak more, except enigmatic sentences.

And so they came, at last, among the big, bleak, northern hills. They had seen nothing of the famous Spotted Antelope, whose party was rumored to be south by the river, waiting to intercept their passage. But the river was many days behind them. They had plunged for four days through the very heart of the Dakota lands, unspied. But on the fifth day they rode over a ridge and came swooping down on four horses and two men at the edge of a creek. So infinitely distant were these Sioux from any thought of danger that they could not believe their eyes until this mysterious Cheyenne charge had scooped them up and made them safe prisoners.

The coups were duly counted; the scalps were promised; but then Rising Hawk determined to extract what kind of information he could from the prisoners.

The first was a stalwart brave of forty-five, hard as iron. He did not stir an eye or abate his contemptuous smile while splinters were driven under his nails and then set on fire. Torridon, transfixed with horror and fear, saw the Cheyennes prepared to take sterner measures and could not stand it. He snatched his pistol out and sent a bullet through the poor fellow's brain.

He half expected that the Cheyennes, their cruel taste once sharpened, would rush on him in a body. To his amazement, they took not the slightest heed of his action. They merely ripped the scalp away from the dead man and turned to the second prisoner. He had borne up as calmly as the other until this moment, but it appeared that the slaughtered warrior was his father. Now his nerves gave way. He was only a lad of fourteen of fifteen, early on the warpath. In another moment he was groaning forth answers to the questions of Rising Hawk.

It was true that Spotted Antelope was far away to the south and not expected for many days. In the meantime, the Sioux village for which the march was aimed had been shifted from its old site to one a little bit more southerly, among the lower hills, between two shallow streams of water. It was a scant half day's march distant. There was no dream of danger threatening among the villagers. They felt that Spotted Antelope was an ample shield between them and the Cheyennes. In conclusion, the youth begged a knife thrust which would end his wretched life, since he had proved a coward and betrayed his people.

Even that mercy was denied him. Rising Hawk felt that something more could be gained, perhaps, from this glib talker. In the meantime, all was as he wished. There were some sixty or seventy braves within the village. One rush should carry it, and after that, there would be the scalps of women and children— cheaply taken, and just as valuable as the scalps of matured warriors.

They pushed on until the evening. Rising Hawk himself, riding in advance, spied on the enemy from the crest of a hill and came back with the report that the Sioux were in their hands. All the village was preparing for the night; the horses were being driven in in the most leisurely fashion. Should they not attack now and overwhelm that town with a single rush?

They turned to Torridon for an answer. He answered simply with an instinct to delay the horror which seemed sure to come. Let them rest throughout the night. They were weary, now, from the long march. In the morning they would be fresh, and the Sioux would be cold with sleep. In the gray dawn the blow should be struck! Rising Hawk submitted to this advice with some grumbling, but he did not appeal from it. It was felt that the mighty medicine of Torridon alone was worthy of credit for having brought them undetected into the heart of the enemy's country, and he was looked upon with great respect.

They pitched their camp at the throat of a blind canyon. It ran straight in toward the heart of the higher hills, and, around the first bend, they camped for the night. The canyon was a pocket which would conceal them from the foe! In the morning they would break out and slaughter!

Wrapped in his blanket, Torridon lay long awake, staring at the distant, cold shining of the stars. He felt weak and small. It was not the cold of the night that made him tremble. And he wished, with closed, aching eyes, for the end of to-morrow, whatever it might bring.

He slept and dreamed that the attack took place and that he himself rode in the forefront, shouting, and that in the village he was slaughtering more than all the rest—slaughtering women and children, until the iron hand of a Dakota warrior fell on his throat. He wakened, half choking. There was a touch on his shoulder.

It was Rising Hawk. All around him stood the shadowy forms of the warriors. The horses had been brought in, soundlessly.

"What has happened?" asked Rising Hawk.

"There is danger," panted Torridon.

"Aye, White Thunder," said the chief. "There is danger. Last night you would not let us strike. Now the time has passed. The Dakota boy has escaped and gone to warn his people! What medicine have you now to give us a victory, White Thunder? Or rather, after all our work, what medicine have you that will take us safely home?"

Torridon got staggering to his feet. Across the sky was stretched a thin, high-riding mist. Behind it rode a young moon. Everything could be half seen, the tall, ragged rocks at the sides of the ravine, the tall gloomy forms of the Cheyenne.

He thought he could see, too, the arrival of the Dakota boy at the village, the mustering of the warriors, and then, what? According to the plan which had been made and which the boy could not have failed to know, the Cheyennes were to wait until morning to attack. What band of Dakotas could hear this plan without determining on a counterstroke? No, they were already out and coming, moving swiftly and softly across the plain—on foot, perhaps, to make sure of greater noiselessness! And then the Sioux would come to the mouth of the ravine—perhaps they were here already, and creeping up, rifles ready, murder in their savage hearts!

Torridon looked wildly around him. How should they escape? The walls went up like perfect cliffs. No horse could mount them. And if the men saved themselves, they would be saved only for the moment. On foot, this vast distance from home, they would be hunted down and speared, like starved wolves!

"What are we to do?" asked Rising Hawk, more harshly. "Do you tremble, maker of medicine?"

Bitterness and mockery were in his voice, and Torridon said in husky answer: "Leave the horses here—go down the ravine— every man softly—every man softly. Do you hear me, Rising Hawk?"

"I hear," said the war chief. "Are we to leave our horses and have them caught—while we—"

That was not the thought in the mind of Torridon, but suppose that they tried to move from the valley on horseback, and gave to the Sioux the huge targets of man and horse together? So he thought and he insisted almost angrily: "Leave the horses here with the boys. Move out with the rifles. Quickly, quickly, Rising Hawk!"

"It was at dawn that we were to take scalps," the chief reminded him, with a voice like a snarl. "Now we shall be lucky if we save our own!"

Nevertheless, he gave the order, and they moved down the canyon slowly, softly. The warriors were both angry and nervous—angry because after all their march they now appeared to be turned back with but a single scalp; nervous because they dreaded any move, no matter how short, without their horses under them.

They passed down the ravine—Torridon in the rear, stumbling, making more noise than all the rest of that shadowy party, for his knees were very loose and wabbly beneath him. Yet they gained the mouth of the ravine unhindered. Not a shot had been fired against them, and the way home across the prairie was open!

He could have shouted for joy, but he was withheld by the fierce rush of another thought upon him. Somewhere across the dimness of the moonshine, surely the Sioux were advancing with all their warriors—their boys left at home with the old men and the women to keep guard against the chance of any counterstroke. Surely they were coming, or else they were unworthy of the name which they had gained in generations of fierce campaigning until all their kind upon the plains trembled at the dreadful name of the Dakotas. Tribe after tribe they had thinned to the verge of extinction; tribe after tribe they had thrust west and south. Their pride and their courage and their self-belief were all equally great.

So they would surely come, to rush the Cheyennes in the throat of the valley. They would come hastily though silently. Once they closed the mouth of that ravine, the Cheyennes to the last man were theirs, and they would make even the late crushing victory of the great Spotted Antelope seem like child's play compared with the slaughter which they would make among the rocks!

So thought Torridon, and then he saw the great opportunity. No rushing of a village. No butchery of women and children. But a stroke of war!

It lay below him so clearly that already he seemed to see the dark figures trooping.

He found Rising Hawk.

"Half on each side of the ravine, among the rocks—scatter the men, Rising Hawk," he advised. "Then wait and wait. The Dakotas are sure to come. They come to trap us, and they will be trapped like fish in a net. Every Cheyenne will be drenched with blood, and there will be scalps in every tepee!"

Rising Hawk hesitated, not from doubt, but because the incoming of that thought numbed him with pleasure. He gave the orders instantly, and the idea spread like fire through the ranks. Despite all discipline and the necessity of silence, a grim murmur ran among the braves. They split into two sections. One rolled to the eastern side of the valley, the other rolled to the western side, and in a trice all sight and sound of them had disappeared among the shrubs, among the splintered rocks.

Even Torridon could hardly believe the ground was alive with such a dreadful little host of trained fighters. But up the valley, from the place where the boys still kept the horses, there was occasionally the sound of a hoof striking against a rock, or the distinct noise of a snort or a cough, as one of the grazing animals sniffed dust up his nostrils.

And now only time could ripen the tragedy and bring it to perfection. But as he lay, he heard a whisper of one warrior to another: "We cannot fail. How can we fail? The Sky People fight for us. They will lead our bullets into the hearts of the Sioux. Hai! We have strong medicine with us this night!"

Torridon found his lips stretching into a stiff and painful smile, and his heart was hot and glad. He had hunted beasts before this day. Now he was a hunter of humans, and his veins were running with hot wine!

CHAPTER VII

★

Victory

The moon was westering fast. The light it cast seemed to grow dimmer, but this was only in seeming and not in fact, for the sky was mottled with a patterning of broken clouds, and in the distance the curve of the river was beginning to be visible, like a streak of smoke across the lower ground.

Torridon began to take sights with his rifle, aiming at rocks on the farther side of the valley, shifting to shadowy bushes, and promising himself that it be difficult work to strike a target by such a light as this.

A light that constantly changed! Yes, when he looked now down toward the river, he saw that it was no longer a strip of smoke, but a width of dull, tarnished silver. Then he understood; the dawn was coming!

He was cold and stiff with lying in one place. Dew clogged his hair and moistened the tips of his ears. But wild excitement made him forget such minor evils. The dawn was coming, the light slowly, slowly, was freshening—and then suddenly out of the lowlands came a troop of figures!

Not see them? They were like black, striding giants through the ground mist. And he could see, faintly, the shimmer of light on their rifles! They had taken long, long to come, but now they were coming swiftly.

He turned his rifle toward them—then remembered that their keen eyes might detect the shining of the steel of the barrel. Hastily he muffled the gun under his robe.

Surely fifty other men among the rocks were making similar

movements, but there was not so much as a whisper of sound. Very well that this was so, for there was no wind. The morning was deathly still, and the sky was turning milk-white with the coming of the day.

Straight on came the Dakotas. With a wildly beating heart Torridon counted them. Forty—sixty—seventy-two striding forms, black as jet through the land mist. Coming rapidly and yet without a whisper of sound!

They grained the throat of the ravine. Let not a Cheyenne move! Another ten strides, and the foe would be in the mouth of the trap!

But in the mouth of the ravine, as though suspicious of the greatness of their luck, the Sioux made a considerable halt, until, up the valley, came the sound of stamping and snorting horses. Then with one accord, no signal or order given, they moved forward, drawn by their lust for horseflesh and their burning hunger for Cheyenne blood. They went with their straight bodies now bent well forward, their rifles swinging, and presently they were well within the gap—

At that instant, a single rifle clanged from the opposite side of the ravine. In the middle of the Sioux band a warrior bounded into the air with a cry which seemed to Torridon the hugest sound that ever left human lips.

Before the dead body reached the ground, fifty rifles had spat fire and the Dakotas went down like toppling grass.

They were all in a close body. If a bullet missed one it was almost sure to strike another. A great shout of woe and terror rose from them, and as it fell, the shrill yell of dying men still hung high in the air. They wavered—then they broke back for the mouth of the ravine. Too late! Loading as they moved, the Cheyennes were slipping from among the rocks. That instant of wavering was costly. Against freshly charged weapons the Dakotas made their rush, and the blast of the second volley withered and curled them up and sent them scampering in plain panic down the valley.

After them went the Cheyennes, for they remembered, now, the horses and the boys with whom their trap had been baited. They rounded the turn of the ravine. The ground was littered with fallen guns, which the enemy had dropped in their flight, and in the growing light the Dakotas could be seen clambering hastily up the sheer walls of the rocks.

There were few loaded weapons to fire after them. But there was enough work to secure those who had not managed to gain the rocks. The fleetest of the Cheyennes had overtaken them and, in the largeness of their hearts, a few prisoners were taken.

Madness took the Cheyennes by the throat. Up and down that ravine men danced and yelled in the fury of their joy. The scalps had been torn from the dead or the dying. The weapons had been gathered, the fallen stripped of clothing.

Before full day showed the real horror of the canyon, Torridon took Ashur and rode him down the valley, the stallion snorting with disgust. At the mouth, facing the brightening lowlands, he waited for the Cheyennes to come after him and begin the southward march. And then it was that temptation swelled big in the heart of Torridon. There was no one near him. Once away, no horse among their numbers could overtake Ashur!

But his promise held him—that and the knowledge that he was deep in hostile country where, in a day or two, scores of man hunters would be on the trail.

So he hesitated, and at last the torrent of warriors poured out around him. Their work was finished. Twenty-six dead men lay in the canyon. Five captives, their feet tied beneath the bellies of ponies, were carried along, and among them—strange chance!— the boy who had escaped from them and given that warning by which the Sioux had been drawn into this dreadful mantrap!

As every man went by Torridon he cast a present or a promise to the white man. Beaded moccasins, hunting knives, a deerskin shirt, even one or two rifles were donated. A spare pony was loaded with these gifts, and well burdened by them.

But this was not all. Rising Hawk was hot to go at once against the Dakota village and strike it while its defenders were away and before those stragglers across the hills could regain the town.

He was dissuaded with difficulty. The way across the high hills was very short. It was certain that the stragglers from the battle already had carried themselves and their tale of woe to the town, and at that very moment the Dakotas were able to throw into the field a greater man power than that of the invaders.

But though dissuaded from an attack, upon one point Rising Hawk had made up his mind. Among his prisoners was a tall youth, wounded through the left calf and bleeding freely in spite of what bandaging they could do. He never could live through a single day of riding. But he was the son of Spotted Antelope, and in the camp of the Sioux, still living and reserved for the return of Spotted Antelope, was Standing Bull. Why not exchange the son of the chief for the big Cheyenne?

They journeyed rapidly around the hills toward the town. Before they saw it, they heard a sound like the noise of a rising wind. It was the many-throated wail from the village! And as they came in view and drew nearer, they heard the noise increasing, a sound that took from the heart of Torridon all the hot pride of victory.

Such a victory never had been before—twenty-six Sioux fallen and five taken, and not a single Cheyenne had been lost!

Yet all the manhood of those stern Dakotas was not broken. Rearmed with every chance weapon they could pick up, the survivors of the late battle, reënforced by old men and young boys, sat their horses in a long line. They were drawn up close to the outer line of the lodges, to be sure, but nevertheless it was plain that they intended to fight their defensive fight, in case of need, in the open field and not from behind shelter. Up and down their ranks rode an old chief, no doubt exhorting them to be of good heart in spite of the disaster.

Rising Hawk sent in the boy who had been captured before. It was only a few minutes that they had to wait. Evidently the son of Spotted Antelope was highly prized in the Dakota camp, and presently the great form of Standing Bull was seen riding out from the village, with an escort of two warriors.

The son of the Sioux chief was sent forward to meet them, likewise accompanied by two Cheyenne warriors. So the parties met. The Cheyennes took their comrade and turned away. The Sioux returned to the village.

And so it was that Torridon clasped hands with Standing Bull again.

The giant Indian made no secret of his joy at finding himself among his friends again, but he declared that he never had had a doubt that his good friend, White Thunder, would devise some means for his delivery. He had been assured in a dream, he vowed, that White Thunder was coming to his aid, with the Sky People. Now it was accomplished.

The happiness of Standing Bull, indeed, was complete. For, having brought Torridon into the tribe and recaptured him after his escape, he felt that everything that was done by the medicine of the white man redounded largely to his credit. In this belief he was not crossed by the remainder of the Cheyennes.

Of the entire party of fifty, there was not a single man who had not at least counted a second or a third coup. And twenty-six scalps hung dripping at their saddlebows. They were enriched with honor, and they had avenged a recent defeat so thoroughly that the whole Cheyenne nation and all the most distant tribes of it would rejoice with them.

Rising Hawk was now a man of note. On the strength of this brilliant action, performed while he was yet wounded from the other battle, he stood fair to succeed High Wolf when that old man at last died or resigned his leadership of the tribe.

As for Torridon, he did not receive so much honor for his suggestion of the trap at the mouth of the ravine. It was rather because he had predicted the time at which they would take scalps. And even for that the regard he received was of a peculiar nature. To be sure he had done well. He had fought with the foremost. But still there was little honor paid to his person. It was to his magic powers that honors were accorded in the most liberal sense. They looked upon him not so much as a brave or wise man but as a peculiar instrument to which the spirits had confided an over-whelming power. He was hardly thought of as an individual at all.

Trusting in that power, straight south rode the war party. If they met with Spotted Antelope they were wildly confident that victory again would be theirs. So Torridon spent anxious days until the river was crossed and at last they entered the comparatively friendly prairie where the power of the Cheyennes ruled.

CHAPTER VIII

★

To Make a Spirit Happy

A treble dignity invested Standing Bull when the war party returned to the village, so that he even could dispute with Rising Hawk the honors and the dignities of the expedition, though all that he had done was to be delivered from the hands of the Dakotas.

But, in the first place, he it was who had brought Torridon to the Cheyennes, and at secondhand, as it were, all the wonders which Torridon had worked since his arrival. Again, Standing Bull had taken prominent part in the first unfortunate expedition against the Sioux and duly counted his two coups before capture. Thirdly, the big man had the credit which comes of entering the jaws of death and escaping therefrom.

When the multitudes poured out from the Cheyenne camp, they yelled the name of Standing Bull louder than all the rest, except for a continual roar which lasted from the time the party was first met by fast-riding young men until the whole band had conducted the warriors to the center of the camp, and the burden of that roaring noise was the name of White Thunder. They called upon him, however, as they would have called upon a spirit. But they called upon Standing Bull as upon a man.

When that warrior returned, therefore, he found all in order with his reputation, but all out of order in his lodge. His favorite wife was a wracked and helpless woman, lying stretched on her bed, too weakened by a debauch of grief that had followed the tidings of the loss of her lord to more than raise her head and smile weakly in greeting. Her shaven head glistened repulsively under

43

the eye of her husband; her body was slashed and torn; her scalp was crossed with many knife slashes; and, beyond this, she had given away practically everything in the lodge and the entire horse herd of her husband in the midst of her grief in order to propitiate the Sky People and to give more lasting rest to the spirit of Standing Bull. In all this, she had acted a most pious part, but it left Standing Bull a beggared man.

For that, he cared not at all. There were many gifts from his friends. White Thunder alone gave ten horses to make a handsome beginning of a horse herd for his old friend, and High Wolf donated a store of provisions. In a day, the lodge was well supplied with all the necessaries. So fluid was prosperity in an Indian tribe! It ebbed and flowed like the sea.

In the meantime, the entire stage was left to be monopolized by Rising Hawk and Standing Bull. White Thunder had withdrawn to his tepee, where he lay on his bed and slept longer than any warrior should, and the whoopings and the yellings only made him turn from time to time and exclaim impatiently.

Young Willow, grown suddenly tender beyond her wont, watched over him. With a new-cut branch she waved the flies away for him, and with ambidextrous skill saw to it that he slept and that food was ready when at last he wakened.

He lolled at east against the most comfortable of his back rests and ate of the meat which was placed before him—not simply dried flesh of the buffalo, but stewed venison, freshly killed, and roasted venison, turned at the fire on a dozen small spits and handed to him bit by bit by the squaw.

With burning eyes of pleasure she regarded the man of the lodge.

"So!" said Young Willow. "You rode out groaning, and you have come back famous!"

"Fame is noise," said Torridon sententiously—and wearily also, for he was still tired from the long ride.

"Noise?" cried Young Willow, growing angry at once. "Fame is all that men live for and all that the dead are remembered by!"

"The people shout to-day, they yawn to-morrow," sighed Torridon.

"Good fame is better than a handsome face," said the squaw.

"It is a breath," said the boy.

"It is to men what their breath is to the flowers," said the squaw.

"The flowers soon wither," said Torridon, "and so what becomes of them?"

"The sweetness they have left on earth is remembered," replied Young Willow.

He felt himself fairly beaten, and acknowledging it by his silence, he smiled almost fondly on that grotesque face, and she smiled back at him, gently.

"From the time we left until the time we returned," said Torridon, "I fired my rifle only twice."

"And then?" she asked him, hungrily.

"Then," he admitted, with a lift of the head, "I saw a Sioux jump his height into the air each time." He added, chuckling: "They must live on springs, because they die in the air!"

Young Willow laughed, like the cawing of a crow.

"That is a good thing to remember," said she. "How many spirits, White Thunder, came down at your call?"

An honest man would have shrugged his shoulders and declared that there was not a spirit in the air on that day of bloodshed. But Torridon had discovered that honesty availed him nothing. If he put all on a common-sense plane, it was simply believed that he was deceiving the people and hiding the truth, and veiling his powers.

He said as gravely as possible: "There was a spirit in front of every man. There were eighty Sioux, and yet all their bullets could not find a single Cheyenne. I shall tell you why; I had placed a spirit in front of every warrior. The ghosts turned the bullets away. Some of those bullets went back and killed the men who had fired them!"

At this prodigy, Young Willow opened her eyes and her mouth. She drank, as it were, of the mystery. Doubt was far from her. This was a story which would thrill the very hearts of the men, the women, and the children, and she could be fairly sure that White Thunder would not tell the story himself. It was in her hands!

Beads and shells would be showered upon her for the telling of such a miracle. In fact her housekeeping for the white man was turning out a sinecure of great value, in her eyes.

"You saw them, White Thunder?" she breathed.

"I alone," said he. "There is a veil before the eyes of other men. A spirit like a great bat flew before Rising Hawk. Bullets glanced from its wings and made sparks of bright red light."

There was a little more of this fantastic conversation. Then, when Torridon went to sleep again, the squaw slipped from the lodge, fairly bursting with her tale. She went back to the tepee of her husband to find that High Wolf was in serious conversation with Standing Bull.

The old chief turned on the squaw with a harsh voice.

"What of White Thunder?" he asked.

She concealed the miracle which had just been confided to her. She preferred to retail it herself to small gatherings.

"He still sleeps."

High Wolf made a gesture of impatience.

"The Sky People have sent us a pig in the form of a man," he declared scornfully. "Has he done no boasting?"

"Only that two Dakotas fell under his rifle."

High Wolf and Standing Bull exchanged glances.

"That is nothing to him?"

"He sleeps again." Young Willow smiled.

"He neither has danced nor sung?"

Young Willow shrugged her shoulders.

"He has had a few Dakotas killed, and taken a few scalps to make the Cheyennes proud. But what is that to him? If he wished, he would wash the Dakotas into the rivers so thickly that the Father of Waters would be choked on his way to the sea. The Cheyennes come home and sing like children over a few beads. White Thunder sleeps so that he may dream of happier things."

The two warriors listened to this speech with the deepest attention.

"He is not happy, then?" asked High Wolf.

"He is as always. I spoke to him about fame. He turned my words into the thinnest air."

High Wolf gestured toward the door, and the squaw departed. After she had gone, High Wolf said: "From the time you first brought him to us, I knew that he was a gift from the heavens. But I never knew until now what his powers could be."

"Use him now, while he is with us," said Standing Bull. "Use him like a magic rifle which will soon be gone. For he is unhappy among us. I cannot tell why, but he is unhappy!"

"I, however, know the reason," returned the chief. "It is because of a woman."

"Ha?" cried Standing Bull. "If it is a Crow, a Blackfoot, if it is even a Sioux, there are enough horses in the tribe to buy ten girls for him."

"Tell me," said the old man. "How often do the whites sell their women?"

Standing Bull made a face of disgust.

"A woman to a white man," he admitted, "is like a child to a mother."

He added: "Is it a white girl?"

High Wolf nodded.

"It is a white girl," he said.

At that, the big man threw out his arms.

"It is she who lives at Fort Kendry. I saw her. She is no bigger than a child. In twenty days she could not flesh a robe. She has no more force in her hands than there is in the claw of a sparrow. Why should a man want her?"

"This is not a man. It is a spirit," said High Wolf.

The warrior made no answer.

"Heammawihio," went on the chief gravely, "has given power to you in this matter. It was you who brought us White Thunder. It was you, also, who followed him to Fort Kendry and brought him to us a second time. Therefore, it is plain that the Great Spirit wishes to work through you in all of these things. Perhaps it was to free you that we were given this last great victory over the Sioux. At any rate, it is clear that you must do what is necessary to keep White Thunder happy—that is, to keep him with us. You must bring to him the white girl that he wants."

Standing Bull groaned.

"Twice in the trap makes a captured wolf," he said.

"Look over the tribe," said High Wolf. "Take the finest horses and the strongest braves, but fix this in your mind: That you must ride to Fort Kendry and bring the girl here!"

CHAPTER IX

★

A Dangerous Task

For a whole week, Standing Bull purified himself every day. It became known throughout the village that he was about to attempt some great and secret thing. For every day he went to the sweat house and there he had water poured over red-hot, crumbling stones until the lodge was filled with choking, blinding fumes. In these he remained for a long time, and then came out staggering and reeling like a drunkard. He would run down the hillside naked, the steam flying up from his body, and plunge into the cold river.

In this manner he was driving out evil and preparing himself for a great deed.

He fasted, also, eating sparingly only once every second day, and he never smoked, except ceremonially. With his hands he touched no weapons. He was much alone, and used to sit on a hill overlooking the camp and the river for hours and hours at a time. Sometimes he was seen there in the midday. Again, the growing dawn light discovered Standing Bull on the hill. Perhaps he was wrapped in a buffalo robe. Perhaps he was half naked, as though unaware of heat or of cold.

His poor wife, Owl Woman, cured by the return of her husband, was up and about the camp, frightfully worried by the procedures of her spouse. She had harried herself until she was a mere caricature of a woman, but she was honored throughout the village because of the extremity of her devotion. Even that harsh and incredulous critic, Young Willow, was heard to say: "She was just a young woman before; now she is beautiful."

"Beautiful?" echoed Torridon, always willing to argue with the squaw.

"No good woman can be ugly," said Young Willow.

Owl Woman, therefore, was seen about the camp anxiously inquiring what could be in the mind of her husband, and then rather naturally she told herself that it was because she had deformed herself so greatly by mourning. She even came to Torridon and brought him a gift of carved bone to ornament a back rest. She wanted to know how she could win back her husband.

He accepted the gift, gave her a simple salve to hasten the healing of the wounds which covered her body, and then told her to go home and cover her shaven head with a mantle, and to be seen singing around the lodge. As for her husband, he assured her that the heart of Standing Bull was not estranged. He simply was having a struggle with spirits.

Common sense, of course, would have dictated all these sayings to any man; but she received them with devout thankfulness. She took the mantle which he gave her and went off with a step so light and swift that the cloth—it was a bright Mexican silk gained from the Comanches—streamed out behind her as she went.

Torridon watched her going until Young Willow broke in on his thoughts with her harsh voice:

"Why do you sneer and smile to yourself after you have given advice to people and showed them the truth? He that scorns others must sit on a cloud!"

On the evening of the seventh day, Standing Bull himself came to Torridon. He looked thin. His eyes were sunken, and his lips were compressed.

"I am going to try to do a great thing," he said. "Give me a charm to help me, White Thunder!"

"There are all sorts of charms," said the young man. "If I gave you a charm at random it might be the worst thing in the world for you. Tell me what you want to try."

"I cannot tell you that," grumbled Standing Bull. "Only—it is something to make you happy!"

"Shall I tell you the quickest way to make me happy?" said

Torridon. "Send away the young men who watch me day and night. Let me have Ashur and one minute to get away from the camp. Then I shall be happy, Standing Bull, but nothing else matters to me!"

"Do you ask me to give away my right hand, White Thunder?" asked the chief gloomily. "Then I must go away and carry no luck from you!"

He departed slowly in a sort of despair.

Then he began to make the round of the camp. His reputation was now so big that he was able to call on six of the best warriors in the village and enlist them to follow him wheresoever he chose to lead them. The desperate nature of the work which he had in mind kept him from revealing the secret. Chiefly because, if it was rumored about the camp and came to the ear of Torridon, he was afraid that the great magician would blast all their plans.

At last he had his party together. There were three horses for every man; the braves were painted for the warpath; and Standing Bull rode with them three times around the village. As he came opposite each of the cardinal points of the compass in making this circuit, he blew smoke offerings, but after the third circle, he bore away to the northwest. They crossed the shallow river, and disappeared over the plains, while Torridon, together with most of the gathered tribe, watched their going.

"Standing Bull is like a buzzard," said Young Willow. "He is always hungry and therefore he is always on the wing."

But Standing Bull was not thinking of fame; he was facing forward to the dreadful difficulty of his task and wishing that, in all the world, some other duty could have been assigned to him. Sometimes he wished that the entire Cheyenne nation could be behind him for the work. But again, he realized that such numbers could do nothing secretly, and at the first approach of an armed tribe all the people who lived outside the fort would retire within its walls—Samuel Brett with his niece among the rest. He realized also that he never had seen the face of the girl. He had seen her only in the dusk, and if there were more than one girl in the house he would be shrewdly put to it to select the right one.

It was no wonder that with these thoughts in his mind he went on the journey with a depressed heart. All the way his words were few, but the warriors followed without a sign of discontent until they came over the lower hills and at last looked down on Fort Kendry.

Then they assembled together and Red Shirt, chief of the followers of the big leader, spoke for the rest.

"Have you come for white scalps, Standing Bull?" he asked with much gravity.

"You perhaps, never have taken one?" said Standing Bull pleasantly. For the entire tribe knew about the long-tressed scalp which hung in the lodge of Red Shirt.

"Because of that scalp I took," said Red Shirt frankly, "I cannot ride into a trading post without fear. For the white men never forget. Because of that scalp, many Cheyennes have died, and now I know that it is better to fight with the Crows or the Blackfeet or the Dakotas, even, than to fight with the white men."

The rest of the men listened in silence which agreed totally with their spokesman, and Standing Bull saw that he would have a good deal of explaining to do.

He said cheerfully: "I, too, my brothers, know that the white men are dangerous. I have not brought you here to take scalps, but to do something still more important. I shall tell you simply, now that you have come to the place where the thing must be done."

He made a pause and swept his hand toward the fort. The rambling group of unpainted walls, some stone built, all rough and carelessly made, the ramshackle roofs, the twisting fence lines, made a very study in confusion. But at the tops of the walls of the fort itself they could see the little round mouths of the cannon which made such miraculous noise and killed at such a miraculous distance.

With equal awe and hate the band looked down upon this stronghold of the whiteskins.

"We do not love these people," said Standing Bull, "but one man with a white skin has done much for the Cheyennes. I speak of White Thunder."

A unanimous grunt of agreement greeted this remark.

"Now, my brothers," said Standing Bull, "we wish to keep White Thunder among us, I am sure. We never have known hunger since he came. He can bring the rain from heaven, and he can turn the bullets of the enemy in battle. He can bring ghosts to protect us and to send our bullets straight into the hearts of our foes. To keep him, we have our young braves guard him. That is hard work. Besides, some day he may find a way to trick our cleverest young men and to escape."

"That is true," said the youngest of the party, a keen stripling of twenty years. "When I guarded him, I trembled with fear. I would as soon try to hold the naked lightning in my hand as to keep White Thunder from doing what he wanted to do."

"But," said Standing Bull, "if once we can make him happy among us, all will be well. And that can be managed, I think. Here in Fort Kendry is the thing that he wants. It is not horses or money or buffalo robes. It is a squaw. There is a girl here whom he loves. Because she is not with him, his heart is sick. Now I, my brothers, hope to catch that girl and take her back to him. You see that our business is not so dangerous as the taking of white scalps."

Red Shirt exclaimed impatiently: "I, Standing Bull, know the white men, and I know that they put more value on their women than they do on their scalps!"

Standing Bull scowled at this opposition.

He said at length, bitterly: "I shall take the chief risk. I cannot make you help me. But if you stay here, I shall go down alone and bring the girl away, or die in that work. I am trying to do something for all the people of the Cheyennes. Who will help me? Let us once bring the girl to White Thunder, and he will stay with us as contentedly as a bird in a nest."

They stared at him, hardly able to believe. Red Shirt suggested that there were pretty maidens among the Cheyennes. But Standing Bull waved him to scorn.

"White Thunder," he explained, "does not think like a man, but like a foolish boy that is sick. We, like parents, must try to please him. Because the boy has been given power."

This simple reasoning appeared conclusive. One and all agreed that they would do their best. If they succeeded, even though they returned without scalps or horses, certainly they would be gloriously received by the Cheyennes. So they loosed their reins and went on toward the fort.

CHAPTER X

★

A Treasure of Great Price

Once before, Standing Bull had gone to Fort Kendry. But though he had come there in the daylight, he had done his work in the night and escaped again under cover of the dark. He had no fear that he would be recognized now, or suspected of any evil intention. To mask the real purpose of his journey, he had seen to it that some of the extra horses were loaded with buffalo robes of good quality. To all intents, they would appear like a small band of warriors who had come in to trade and get what they could. In the meantime, they would look around them for the girl.

They hardly had come into the village before they were welcomed. The more important traders had their quarters within the fort itself, where they worked for the fur company. But in the village were independents who picked up a little business here and there from just such small parties as these. As the Cheyennes entered, wrapped to the eyes in their robes, their long rifles balanced across the pommels of their saddles, first one and then another agent greeted them fluently in their own tongue and tempted them with bottles of whisky. Both of these, Standing Bull passed by, but a third man he followed into his booth and looked at the display of goods. There were beads of all kinds, together with hatchets, knives, tobacco, tea, sugar, coffee, flour, calico, clothes and ribbons of staring colors, blankets and a hundred little foolish trinkets. Standing Bull himself was enchanted by the appearance of some little bells which, as the agent pointed out, could be tied in the mane of the horse, or in the hair of the warrior.

"So," said Standing Bull to Red Shirt, "a brave would be

known before he was seen. His friends would be glad. He would walk with music!"

And he jangled the bells. But Red Shirt was entirely absorbed in the contemplation of a jug of whisky; the pungent fragrance of it already was in his nostrils.

However, nothing would be done, no matter what the temptation, until Standing Bull gave the signal, and certainly he would not give such a signal on this day. The number of the robes was small, barely large enough to excuse their offering in trade, after so long a journey to present them. On the first day there should be no trafficking. Indeed, if possible, Standing Bull intended to get his party away from the fort before the warriors had tasted the unnerving fire of the whisky. One bottle of that would be enough to start a debauch which would ruin all plans.

In the midst of all this confusion, while the trader and his boy were panting with eagerness for plunder, another form appeared, a tall and magnificently made frontiersman, garbed in the finest of deerskin, heavily beaded, with his long, blond hair flowing down about his shoulders.

A pistol in one side of his belt balanced in a heavy knife which was in front; an in his hands he carried a long, heavy rifle, using it as lightly as though it were a walking staff. He went straight to Standing Bull and raised a hand in greeting.

"How!" grunted the Cheyenne in response.

"How!" said the other cheerfully, and speaking the Indian tongue well enough. "Men tell me that you are Standing Bull, the chief of the Cheyennes?"

Standing Bull wanted nothing so little as to be recognized. He maintained a grim silence and looked the other in the eye.

The white man continued: "We have heard of you. The Dakotas have been here. They had something to say of you and your big medicine!"

Here the boy interrupted: "Hey, you! Are you gonna try to swipe these half-wits out of our booth? Back up, will you, and let us finish our trade with them, or else we'll—"

His employer silenced him with a back-handed cuff that sent the youngster staggering. "It's Roger Lincoln, you little fool," he said, and added: "Glad to see you, Mr. Lincoln!"

Now, at that name there was a little stir among the Cheyennes. In fact, it was known from the Dakotas to the Kiowas and Comanches, over the length and breadth of the plains. They moved back a little, partly as though they did not know what to expect, and partly as if they wanted a better chance to examine and admire the white man. They found him perfect in his appointments, from his hat to his beaded moccasins. Except for the whiteness of his skin—and that was weather-browned enough—he might have stepped into the ranks of any Indian tribe of the plains, a chief, or the favored son of some rich brave.

"I have a house close by," said Roger Lincoln. "I do not wish to make a trade with a friend. I wish to talk to you about better things than buffalo robes. Will you come?"

He added to the trader a brief sentence, promising that he would not barter for a single one of the robes or any other possession of the Cheyennes. The trader, biting his lip, nodded, and watched in silence while the troop filed off at the heels of Lincoln.

The latter took the Indians to his own trading booth a short distance away, and there he seated them in a circle in his room and offered them tea, sweetened with heaps of sugar. With loud smackings, the red men tasted it, rolled their eyes, and poured down the scalding hot tea. They held out their cups for another service, and again the cups were filled brimming. A pipe was passed. Good humor began to possess Standing Bull, greater than the doubt and suspicion in which he had stood when the white man first greeted them. He waited for the meaning of this to be expounded, and presently the meaning was made clear.

"Now, my friend," said Roger Lincoln, "look around you at everything. You see rifles here and pistols there. Here are some barrels of powder. There is lead for making bullets. There are some bullet molds. Here are some knives. See them! Take this one for a present and feel its edge. Also, there are saddles and bridles. Here you see the clothes. There is enough red cloth to put a headband around the head of every Cheyenne—man, and woman, and child! There are beads in these boxes. And here is a little chest stored with all sorts of wonderful things. Back in this corner you can see the hatchets and the axes."

The nostrils of Standing Bull fanned out and quickly contracted as he drew in an envious breath.

"The white men," he said, "are rich. The Indians are very poor."

"Nevertheless," said Roger Lincoln quickly, "they are men, and a man is worth more than you can put on his back or into his hands."

Standing Bull smiled, touched with pleasure almost in spite of himself.

"Perhaps it is true," said he.

"Have you looked at all these things?" asked Lincoln.

"I have seen them very well."

"But look at them again. Examine them. Feel them with your hands. Try the weight of this ax. You see that it has a tooth which will never grow dull, and that hatchet was made to sink into the brainpan of a Dakota."

Standing Bull sighed with a great delight.

"Here, also, are buttons brighter than silver to put along the edges of your trousers. Here are some coils of rope, and look at these iron tent pegs. You know how they are used? And here is an iron-headed hammer which never will break."

The Indians followed every word with intense pleasure and interest.

"Come back with me," went on Roger Lincoln.

He led the way out of the shack and in the rear a large corral opened. In it were fifty or sixty horses to which an attendant was forking out well-cured hay.

"You have the eye which sees horses," said Roger Lincoln. "When you look at these, you will see that they are not like the other horses of the plains. They are taller. Their legs are longer and stronger. They are cross bred. They are not soft like other horses of white men. They are out of plains ponies by fine stallions. Mounted on such horses as these, Standing Bull, you would sweep away from an enemy. You could strike and fly off again out of danger like a hawk playing with a buzzard."

The Cheyennes devoured those horses with greedy looks. It was true that they understood horseflesh perfectly, and now they proved it by the red-eyed silence in which they observed these animals.

After this, Roger Lincoln went on slowly and impressively: "I am not a rich man, my friends. I have worked many years, and what you have just seen is what I have saved. I have paid for these things with blood, you may be sure. I had hoped that with them I could trade and make more money. At last I could go back among my people and sit quietly in a pleasant lodge by the side of a stream, with trees around me, and take a squaw, and raise man children.

"But dearer than peace and happiness are the life and the happiness of a friend. Do you hear me, Standing Bull? You have in your lodges a man with a white skin, and you call him White Thunder. Is it true?"

He said the words as one who puts a statement in question form for the sake of politeness. The Cheyenne leader stiffened a little. His keen eyes turned gravely upon the other, and he said nothing.

"For that man," said Roger Lincoln, "if you will bring him in safety to Fort Kendry, I will pay you everything that your eyes have seen. If you find anything more, you are welcome. I will give you also even the house in which you find all these things and everything down to the ground on which it stands. I have promised. No man has heard me say the thing which is not so!"

This speech made a vast impression upon the Cheyennes. They drew back a little, murmuring, and among the companions of Standing Bull there was only one opinion. Such a princely offer of dazzling wealth should be accepted at once. Never had they seen such riches heaped together! The whole tribe would be rejoiced!

Standing Bull simply replied: "He is not ours to sell. The Sky People sent him to us and if we let him go, they will send us bad luck. Besides, High Wolf never would sell him. And who but a fool, after all, would give up a power that can turn the bullets of the Dakotas as if they were pebbles thrown by children? Do not talk foolishness any more. Besides, Roger Lincoln is a wise man. Would he pay such things except for a man who is worth twice as much? If White Thunder is worth so much to the whites, he is worth ten times more to us!"

He turned to the big, white man and shook his head solemnly:

"Our eyes have not seen White Thunder," said he. "We do not know about what you are speaking!"

CHAPTER XI

★

Children in Trouble

Those men who early went to the Western frontier were, almost without exception, children. Great-shouldered, hard-handed, often hard-hearted children, but nevertheless, children they were. Nothing but childish reasoning could have induced them to leave the cities and the comfortable lands east of the Mississippi for all the chances, the labor, the dangers of the prairie, except that in their heart of hearts they loved a game more than they loved anything else.

So it was with Roger Lincoln. Well-born, well-educated, calm-minded, brave as steel and as keen, he could have had the world at his feet, if he had chosen to live among the civilized. But rather than his knowledge of books he preferred to use his knowledge of the wilderness. Rather than his knowledge of civilized society he preferred to use his knowledge of the barbarians. A fine horse was more to him than a learned companion, and a good rifle better than a rich inheritance.

Stately, gentle, soft of voice, beautiful of face, and mighty of hand, he looked the type of some Homeric hero. There was no cloud of trouble on his brow. His eye was as clear as the clearest heavens.

And yet beneath all this there was the heart of a child. It began to work in him now that he heard the lying reply of Standing Bull. His lips trembled and then compressed. His breast swelled. An almost uncontrollable passion enthralled Roger Lincoln, and the Cheyennes drew a little closer together, overawed and frightened.

"I have been to the Cheyennes a good friend," said Roger

Lincoln. "There are many in your tribe who know that I never have harmed them. Your own chief, High Wolf, remembers a day on the waters of the Little Bender when the Crows were closing around him and there was no hope of help. On that day he was glad that Roger Lincoln was his friend and a friend to the Cheyennes. I split the Crows as a child splits a twig. They ran away, and the Cheyennes followed them and took a great many scalps. There were other days of which I could speak. I have kept the Cheyennes from trouble whenever I was near them. I respected them and thought that they were men and truth speakers. When they came to a trading post where I was, I saw that the traders did not cheat them. I used to stand up in the councils of the white men and say that no matter what they thought of the other red men of the plains the Cheyennes were real men and brave men and that they spoke the truth.

"Because I thought all these things, to-day I was willing to do more than is just. My dearest friend is among your lodges. You keep him there. His heart is breaking. What wrong had he done you or any other Indian? He was young and had harmed no one. He was my friend. I have no other friend half so dear to me as this White Thunder. But you stole him and kept him, after he had done good to one of you. I do not want to name the warrior whose life he saved on the island at the forking of the river. I would not like to say that any man would be so base as to betray the friend who saved him. And yet this is what happened.

"I did not want to talk of these things. Instead, I offered to make a bargain with you. I offered you a ransom. What do you do when a most hated enemy is taken in battle? If his friends offer you horses and guns, you take them and set him free. But you did not take White Thunder in battle. You tricked him into coming to your camp and, after that, you surrounded him with guards. You threatened to kill him if he did not work great medicine for you! And all that I say is true! Now you will not take such a ransom as never was offered to Cheyennes before!

"You forgot the wrong you have done to White Thunder. Instead of keeping him, you should cover him with presents. You

should give him whole herds of horses, and then you should set
him free.

"Or when Roger Lincoln asks, because of the good I have done
for you, you should set White Thunder free even if he had killed
one of your chiefs. But he has killed no one and he has done you
no harm. Only out of the wickedness of your hearts you are
keeping him to be a slave to you, to bring rain to your crops and
make medicine against the other Indians.

"Now, I tell you that you will come to a day when you will
groan at the thought of White Thunder. You will tremble when his
name is mentioned. You will wish that you had starved of hunger
without corn rather than that he should have been kept in the tribe
like a prisoner.

"I tell you this, and when I speak it is not the whistling of the
wind.

"I have been your friend. Now I am your friend no longer.
From the moment that you leave Fort Kendry I am your enemy;
and you shall pay for the evil that is in you. This is my token of
what I will do and of how much I hate you!"

There was a big chopping block near by and in it was stuck a
splitting ax—an old and rusted blade with a wide bevel, useless
for felling tress but acting like a wedge to tear open sections for
firewood. This ax the frontiersman caught up. His childish fury
had reached its climax and with fury in his eye he swung the ax
and cast it from him.

With one hand he had wielded its heavy mass and it spun lightly
away and drove its blade into a post of the corral. So heavy was
the shock that the whole fence trembled. And the bright eyes of
the Cheyennes flashed at one another.

That blow would have driven the ax head well nigh through the
body of a warrior!

"Go!" said Roger Lincoln, and before the wave of his hand the
Indians drew back.

They filed through the store. They reached the street and turned
down it, still walking one behind the other, their muffling robes
high about their faces. They took their horses with them to the
edge of the town and there they sat down in a clearing in a circle.

Standing Bull took out a pipe bowl of red catlinite. This he
filled with tobacco, mixed with dried, powdered bark to make it
burn freely and give pungency to the taste. He fitted in the long
stem and lighted the mixture. He blew a puff to the earth spirits.
He blew a puff to the cardinal points. Then he held up the pipe to
the Great Spirit and chanted slowly a sacred song which, rudely
translated, ran somewhat as follows:

> Heammawihio, lord of the air,
> We are not even master of the ground;
> But we are your children, and we are in
>   trouble!

In this last line the entire band joined, singing like a chorus,
singing heavily:

> Heammawihio, your way is the way of the
>   eagle;
> Our way is the way of the prairie dog,
>   creeping in holes.
> But we are your children, and we are in
>   trouble!

> Heammawihio, your eye sees all things and
>   all thoughts.
> But even in the sunlight our eyes are dark-
>   ened.
> But we are your children, and we are in
>   trouble.

> Heammawihio, for your enemies you keep
>   the polished spears of the lightning;
> And we have nothing but our weak hands
>   with which to strike.
> But we are your children, and we are in
>   trouble.

Give us good council; open our minds; be
        pitiful;
We have no words or thoughts, except to
        pray to you;
But we are your children, and we are in
        trouble.

Between the verses of this solemn song, Standing Bull had
smoked a few puffs from his pipe.

Now it was handed around the circle. Each man smoked. Each
man was silent. When the pipe was empty, the ashes were
knocked from the bowl, and then the council began, Standing Bull
inviting all to speak who had an idea that might be of service in
their present difficulty.

Red Shirt was eloquent at once. His thought was of immediate
and complete surrender. From White Thunder, as he said, the
Cheyennes had received many services. They could make no
repayment for the rain he had brought to them, the Dakota scalps
which he had placed in their lodges, or the members of the tribe
whom he had saved from sickness. It was fitting, therefore, that
they should set the white man free. The additional argument was
that of Roger Lincoln's enmity. Certainly they should set White
Thunder free at any rate. In addition, they had great treasures
offered to them by Roger Lincoln. And, beyond this, there was
now thrown into the scale the terrible hostility of this famous
warrior. It would be far better at once to return to Roger Lincoln
and propose amity. He, Red Shirt, had hardly been able to keep
his tongue quiet when he had heard the magnificent proposals of
the white hunter refused.

After him spoke Rushing Wind, the same who had made the
wager with Torridon about the crossing of the river. He was
equally hot on the other side. What treasures, he asked, could be
offered by any man to offset the magic powers of White Thunder?
He, Rushing Wind, had seen the great enchanter at work. He had
seen spirits called down from the air in the form of hawks. He had
seen the work those spirits could accomplish. White Thunder
knew the language of bird and beast. He could draw the buffalo

out of the plains and bring them close to the village. Everything was possible to him. He was a treasure in himself beyond price. As for Roger Lincoln, he was one man. What could one man perform against the entire Cheyenne nation?

If only, then, they could get what they came for and win the squaw who would keep the enchanter happy, they could wish for nothing else! The medicine of White Thunder would be turned against Roger Lincoln himself and soon that famous scalp would dry in the lodge of a Cheyenne. He, Rushing Wind, hoped that he would be the lucky man. At least, he was not afraid.

This speech of a headlong youth was received in silence. Only the eyes of the older warriors turned gravely to one another, exchanging a thought.

Finally, Standing Bull said, though gently: "No white man ever is alone. Roger Lincoln is a name that can gather a tribe of white warriors. Because I am leading this party, now I must think deeply and pray to Heammawihio for guidance. For myself I wish nothing. I am doing all this for the sake of our people. I shall pray with a pure heart. May I receive guidance!"

He filled his pipe. The others withdrew softly from about him.

CHAPTER XII

★

Through the Smoke

When night came down upon the camp of the Cheyennes, where they had improvised some comfort in the woods, they found that the clement weather had changed much for the worse. The moon for which they hoped did not appear. Instead, the sky was covered with deep gray clouds in the evening, and as the darkness began, the rain commenced also, falling small and soft, but gradually penetrating their clothes with wet and cold. The trees gradually were drenched with moisture. A heavy pattering began in the woods that sounded like the fearless striding to and fro of wild beasts. The fire burned small, with much smoke and little heat, as all the fuel was soaked that they threw into the heap. There was small comfort for them. They were in a far land. They were close to the power of the white men. And their hearts were heavy with the knowledge that they had done wrong, and were contemplating a greater evil.

For, as the darkness came thick, and the rain began to descend, Standing Bull had advanced from among the woods and announced that after consulting the Great Spirit with all his heart he could not understand any message, and therefore he took it for granted that they should continue with the work on which they had come.

That evening he would look over the situation. As for the rest of the warriors, he recommended to them that they earnestly pray that a dream might be sent to one of them suggesting the proper course for the war party.

With that, Standing Bull left them and slipped away among the woods and among the scattering houses until he came close to the square-built log cabin of Samuel Brett.

Here he began to prowl with the greatest caution. The cold of the rain, driven to the bone by occasional flurries of rain, he quite disregarded. He moved in the darkness as though he had been moving in the open light of day, and trying to make his approach unnoticable under the battery of a hundred suspicious eyes. From rock to rock, from bush to bush, he worked softly, until he came close to the house.

After that, he worked back and forth under the wall. By the kitchen door he paused and smelled cookery. He was hungry, and the odors tempted him. There were such fragrances as he never before had connected with food!

However, he banished this passing weakness at once. Completing his tour of investigation, he found two windows, but both were closed and darkened against the night and the rising storm.

He came back to the kitchen door, and pressed close to it. It was a work of some danger. There were considerable cracks in this homemade door, and through the cracks ran long fingers of light which traveled far into the night and showed the rain sifting down steadily. In addition, those fingers of light must be touching his person, and if any one were abroad to watch him, he surely would be revealed.

However, it was necessary for him to learn something of what was inside the house. So he put his eye to crack after crack until through one of the apertures he was able to see the corner which included the stove and the sink.

Two women were there washing tins and dishes. One washed. One dried.

He could see the face of her who dried. She was young, slender, dark of eye and skin. She was pretty enough to have caused the heart of a young brave to leap. Doubtless it was she whom White Thunder wanted.

As for her who washed, her back was turned. She was doubtless the squaw of the house. Yet her back was not flat and broad. The nape of her neck was delicately rounded. However, the squaws among the whites were not like the squaws among the Indians.

He waited, listening.

Their voices were like the sounds of two brooks running through a still woodland, bubbling, and often running together with laughter. Those sounds were pleasant to the ear of Standing Bull. But he thought of the strong-handed squaws in his tepee. He thought of Owl Woman, who nearly had slain herself in the intensity of mourning for her lost lord.

Then his mind grew more contented. To each people, their own women. But his own women were the best in the world, he was sure. Besides, one of them had given him a male child so that the memory of Standing Bull should be kept strong and his spirit alive among men.

At last, she who washed turned from the sink.

The heart of Standing Bull sank!

She was as young as the other. She was younger. Her hair was not dark, but light. The radiance from the lamp shone through it, making it glisten at the outer edges. Her cheek and throat were as sleek as the cheek and throat of a baby. She had large, dim eyes. They did not dance and sparkle like the eyes of the darker girl. There was not much life in this paler creature. And, therefore, doubtless White Thunder could not have chosen her.

However, he who is wise reserves his judgment. Standing Bull reserved his.

Who, after all, can step inside the mind of the white man and be sure of his thoughts? He lives by contraries. The creature will fight, but he cares nothing for the glory of the counted coup, or the symbol of the scalp. He fights to destroy bodies. The red man understands that there is no true death except to the spirit! And so in all things, the white man, in spite of his medicine and his wisdom, lives by contraries, doing foolish things.

Therefore, it might be that White Thunder would prefer this paler girl, this dim-eyed, sad-faced creature.

But why, after all, should she be sad?

Something stirred at the edge of the woods. Instantly, Standing Bull was close down at the foot of the wall of the house, where the darkness covered him. Footsteps came up to the door, a big man was seen there, striped by the light which shone through the cracks. He thrust the door open.

As the door closed upon him, gay voices broke out. There was laughter. Standing Bull understood not a word, but very well he recognized the sound of rejoicing.

Then he crept back to his place of espial and stared through again. The big man had placed on the floor the body of a young deer which he had carried upon his shoulders. Now he sat at a table near the stove—a powerful fellow with huge shoulders and a stern face. His clothes were beginning to steam. A white squaw, older than the two girls, came hurrying in to him. They exchanged words. Her hands were full of cloth, and with it she returned to the other room. The dark-eyed beauty went with her and left the paler girl behind.

She, as was right, tended the hunter. The fragrance of coffee made the air sweet and pungent. There was the scent of frying venison, and the meat hissed and snapped as the heat seared it. Bread was brought forth. It glistened white as snow as the knife of the girl divided it. She laid the food before the hunter. The mouth of Standing Bull watered and he swallowed hard.

Swiftly the hunter ate, and hugely. Like a starved brave returned from the arduous warpath he devoured his food.

Then he leaned back in his chair and lighted a pipe.

Oh, white man, are there no spirits in your world? Without ceremony, brutally, crudely, he filled and lighted the pipe. He leaned back in his chair, chewing the short stem, shifting it from side to side in his white, strong teeth.

As he smoked, he talked. The girl was washing dishes again. Tobacco smoke filled the air. A heavy, thick, sweet odor, unlike that of Indian tobacco.

The hunter drew the smoke into his lungs. It poured forth at his mouth and his nose as he talked. His words became living images in smoke. They rose and melted slowly and flattened against the ceiling.

Standing Bull watched, fascinated. He felt the muscles tightening along his spine. He bristled as a dog bristles, when a strange animal comes near. And Standing Bull, out of instinct, fumbled the haft of his big hunting knife. That rough blond scalp would look very well in the lodge!

The man inside now spoke and beckoned, and the girl stood before him.

Was she his daughter? Was she his youngest squaw?

No, the white man kept only one squaw, for in all things his ways were the ways of ignorance. It was even said, a wonder not to be believed—that sometimes he helped the women in their work around the lodge!

Now the girl stood before the big man. He put out his hand and laid it on her head, and her head bowed a little, as though under a weight.

He spoke to her. His rough voice was softened. His gesture indicated that he talked of some far thing. He shook his head and denied that far thing. Then he appeared to argue. He talked with gestures of both hands. He was eager. Almost he was appealing.

To all of this talk the girl replied with short answers. A brief word. A syllable.

Presently tears began to run down from her eyes.

They fell on her round, bare arms. They fell on her hands, which were folded together. She was not talking at all, and indeed she did not seem even to be hearing what the big hunter said. Her eyes looked off at that distant thing of which they had been speaking before. They were sad eyes. They were like blue smoke. Looking at them, Standing Bull sighed a little.

Suddenly the white hunter jumped up from the table and threw his hands above his head. Standing Bull grinned, for he expected the blow to fall on the girl, but instead, the white man struck his own head and then rushed from the room.

But still the young squaw paid no attention. She was still looking into the distance, still weeping. She sank into a chair. Her head fell against the wall. Her eyes closed. She wept no longer. She was as one whom grief has sickened past tears.

Then by revelation Standing Bull knew what he should have known before. This was the girl!

Dim of eye she was now; but it is happiness which lights a woman, as fire lights a branch and the branch lights the forest.

She wept, and she was in sorrow for the sake of a man who was far away, and that man was White Thunder. It was all clear, clearer than any story told in pictures, though an old sage were at hand to explain their meaning.

Standing Bull slipped away through the woods and rejoined his anxious companions. He came among them with a glistening eye, but he said not a word. Much that was done on distant trails was better left untold until one returned to the village. For what was described to the trail, that was remembered, but what was unnamed at the time, afterward could be expanded.

He closed his eyes. He was regardless of the smoke from the fire which was pouring into his face. Somehow, he would be able to turn this night's adventure and the real peril he had endured into a story of some worth. He was sure of that, if only he could have patience. He would invent; it needs time to search the spirit!

Then, by dim degrees, his thoughts turned back to the white girls. He tried to think of the one of the dancing eyes. But instead, all that he had in mind was the eyes of the other, like blue smoke, covered with sorrow.

He wondered greatly how she would appear if she saw White Thunder. Was not White Thunder even as the girl? There was a veil over his eyes, also. Partly of thought and magic, partly of grief.

Standing Bull no longer wondered that his friend the white magician sorrowed for this girl. He was himself beginning to understand that there is other beauty than that found in red skins. The taste of it, like the taste of a strange and delightful food, entered the soul of Standing Bull.

He stood up. Rather, he leaped to his feet with a grunt that startled his companions out of slumber.

"What is wrong?" asked Red Shirt.

"Nothing," said the leader. "But the fire is all smoke, and the evil ghosts are throwing it into my face."

CHAPTER XIII

★

A Bold Plan

Big Samuel Brett hardly had settled to his second pipe and the narration of the day's hunting when a hand struck at the door. He went to open it, cautiously, one hand ready to thrust it home again and the other hand occupied with his rifle.

"It's Roger Lincoln," said a voice from the rain.

The door twitched wide, instantly, and Roger Lincoln came in, glistening with the wet, his deerskins soaked through and blackened.

"You been swimming in it, it looks like," said Samuel Brett. "Come in and dry yourself out at the stove."

Roger Lincoln waved his hand.

"I've been stalking," he said.

"Deer?"

"Indians."

Brett whistled. His eyes widened, and then drew into the shadows of his brows.

"Where?"

"The trail came here."

"To Fort Kendry?"

"To your house."

"It's that darned drunk Crow with the crooked nose!" suggested Samuel Brett.

"It's a tall Cheyenne by the name of Standing Bull. He was watching through your door."

"I got nothing to do with the Cheyennes. Never traded with them, worse luck!" said Brett.

"They want something to do with you, however. That fellow was very curious."

"Every Indjun is half wolf," said Brett easily. "They gotta go snoopin' and sniffin' around. Why didn't you collar him?"

"My hands are off that gang until they leave the fort. I've told them so. After they start, the knife is out!"

"With the Cheyennes? You could've picked an easier job. Ah, then I understand! It's young Torridon?"

"It is."

The face of Samuel Brett darkened.

"You're wrong again, Lincoln. There never was a Torridon that wasn't a snake and deserved to be treated the same as a snake! And if—"

The hand of Lincoln was raised again, and Brett shrugged his shoulders.

"I shouldn't talk that way. I've tried to argue you out of it before, Roger. But if the kid showed a white face to you, he'll show a black face before you're through with him. I know the breed!"

"Perhaps you do," said Roger Lincoln a little coldly. "But I've not stopped in to talk about Torridon. I've come to tell you that a hard-headed, hard-handed Cheyenne brave is watching you. Why, I don't know, but I don't think he's going to do you much good. Man, watch your house!"

He said it with gravity, and the other nodded assent.

"I'll get Murphy's dog, to-morrow, and keep it around. He's a maneater, that brute. And Pat offered him to me."

"Take the dog by all means—and sleep light! Good-by."

He was gone, in spite of the hospitable protests of Brett. The door closed. Roger Lincoln went back toward his house with a mind filled with misgivings.

Samuel Brett, however, was not alarmed. He had lived all his days in the midst of danger. That which is too well known is apt to be taken too lightly.

To be sure, when he went to bed that night he saw that the door was well secured, and that his rifle and two pistols were at hand near by him. But after that he slept profoundly, and the rumble of his snoring filled the house.

The night grew wilder and wilder. Before morning, the Cheyennes in their clearing had been forced up from their blankets, and

they huddled around a newly built fire, removing to the shelter of
the trees. It was only a mock shelter. The heavy rain, driven far in
through the foliage by the whip of the wind, came sluicing down
upon them in quantities. Over their heads the storm yelled and
roared, and the day came slowly upon them.

They prepared a meal of a few mouthfuls. When it was eaten,
they smoked a pipe with some difficulties. And then Standing Bull
asked for dreams.

Yellow Man was the only one who could oblige. He declared he
had dreamed that he was back in the Cheyenne village and that, in
the middle of the night, he had stepped outside his lodge.

Suddenly the night had become terribly dark. All was blackness.
A wind hooted in his ears like an owl. And when he stumbled back
toward the lodge, it was gone. He ran here and there. He could find
nothing, though his tepee stood in the center of the camp.

At last a star began to shine. He found that he was alone in the
midst of a great plain. Nothing was near him. There was no village
in sight. It was as though the wind had blown him to a great distance!

He dropped to the ground, thereby hoping to see something
against the horizon. Something he did see. It was a tree standing
on a hill. The star was right behind it, and, indeed, the star was in
the middle of it. From the distant heavens, straight through that
tree or ghost of a tree, the star was shining.

This was the dream of Yellow Man. Let who could interpret it!

This strange story was received in silence. But when Yellow Man
left the circle, a little later, Red Shirt remarked with a grunt: "My
blood is cold, brothers, and I think that when we come to the lodge
of Yellow Man, we will find the women and children wailing in it!"

There was no further comment, but all the braves had the same
gloomy thought. Red Shirt insisted that this was a token that they
should give up the attempt which they had in mind. Even if peace
was not made with Roger Lincoln, it would be best to try nothing
more, but to make the best and quickest way back to the village on
the prairie.

Standing Bull answered, logically enough, that a dream in
which a village disappeared and a star shone through the ghost of
a tree might mean a great deal to Yellow Man, but it hardly had

significance for the rest of the party or their work. He had made up his mind. They would attempt what they had come for!

That day, the storm still held, growing momently more violent. They could hear the roaring of the river, swollen with a great voice. And during the day, they went down to trade off their buffalo robes. Under the keen eye of Standing Bull and against his express admonition, they did not dare to take whisky in exchange. And in the evening they went back to their camping grounds with a load of ammunition, a few knives, many trinkets and beads.

When the darkness came on, Standing Bull made his further preparations. Two of the men were to keep the bulk of the horses at the edge of the woods, prepared to rush them into the prairies on a moment's notice. The remaining four, and Standing Bull himself, were to go back with chosen ponies—and one extra mount!—to the vicinity of the house of Samuel Brett.

There, a pair of the warriors would keep the animals at the edge of the trees, taking what care they could that the ponies should not neigh or make any noise of tramping or fighting. Then, accompanied by Red Shirt and Rushing Wind—specially chosen for this purpose by Standing Bull as being the keenest of the band which accompanied him—the leader would go toward the house and try to take the girl from it, in silence if he could, by force and slaughter of the rest of the household if necessary!

The others listened to the plan in silence. They saw that it was desperately bold. The explosion of a gun and a single shot would be enough to bring out the rest of the settlers, gun in hand. But not one of the braves would draw back from his leader in such a time of need. Certainly Rushing Wind and Red Shirt did not know fear!

All was done as had been planned; the horses were established under the trees which stood nearest to the house, and then Standing Bull began to approach, taking the lead, as was his right and his duty.

He went forward crouching, shifting from bush to rock, and rock to bush, and gradually working his way closer. He had covered most of the distance when there was a snarl and then a furious barking just before him.

He heard the rush of a dog through the darkness!

CHAPTER XIV

★

Something Wrong

There was no better watchdog in the world than that borrowed man-killer which now was lunging at the Indian. His was a crossed breed. He was mastiff, boar hound, and wolf, mixed discreetly. He had the cunning power of a wolf, the wind of a hound, and the grip of a mastiff, together with the heart of the latter dog.

He was as good as half a dozen armed guards to keep off strollers and the overcurious, because men do not like to face the danger of a dog bite. The bite may only break the skin; but the broken skin is apt to lead to hydrophobia. Who can tell?

Standing Bull never had seen that dog before. He did not need to see him clearly, however, to realize what was coming. The monster charged through the whipping rain. Straight at him came the dog, with a savage, brutal intaken breath of satisfaction.

At the last instant the Cheyenne twisted on his side. A snake could not have moved more quickly. The dog shot past, trying in vain to check its impetus, and as it went on, Standing Bull drove his hunting knife through the heart of the creature.

There was no sound. The dog fell limply, and Standing Bull wiped off the blade of the knife, listening intently as he did so.

Nothing stirred in the house. He could only trust that the sudden cessation of the growling of the big animal would not rouse suspicions in the house. And so far nothing indicated that they were on their watch. They had consigned their safety into the keeping of one power. That power now was removed, and

Standing Bull felt that perhaps swift success would crown his work.

His two attending shadows drew close to him. They did not congratulate him on the deed he had just performed, but congratulation did not need to be spoken. Standing Bull felt that the very air was electric with the admiration of his friends.

Therefore he went on swiftly to the door. It was the one weak point of the house, being thin and, as already noted, full of cracks. It was the hope of Standing Bull that a little work with a sharp knife might so enlarge one of the cracks that he could reach the latch bar and open the door without more ado.

He worked rapidly, but with the greatest care. Even the squeak of a heavily pressed knife in wet wood might be enough to catch the ear of a sleeper and undo all that had been accomplished up to this point.

Presently, when the soft wood had yielded sufficiently, he thrust the point of the blade through the crack and worked it upward. It clicked on iron, the iron stirred, and with a slight creak of the hinges, the door sagged inward.

Big Standing Bull crouched on the threshold, his heart thundering in his breast like a charge of wild buffalo. But still nothing stirred in the interior. Neither the breath of fresh air entering, full of the dampness of the rain, nor the sound of the door turning on the hinges had been enough to disturb the slumberers—or were they waiting among the shadows all this while, smiling to themselves, their guns ready as soon as the door, like the mouth of a trap, had admitted sufficient victims?

Even on the verge of entering, Standing Bull thought of all these things, and hesitated. But something had to be done. The rain beat like hammers on the surface of the ground. It rattled on his own broad shoulders so loudly that he could have sworn that a whole tribe would have been alarmed by such a noise.

In through the door he went, and moved hastily to one side. The other two followed him. He could hear them breathing, and the faint creaking of a leather jacket as its wet folds were drawn tight at each inhalation.

He got from his knees to his feet, but when he made a step, the water squelched and hissed in his moccasins. He had to pause again, listening with the rigidity of a statue, and then he sat down and dragged off the moccasins. In his naked feet he proceeded with greater ease.

First he went to the stove and from this took out a half-burned stick of wood. There was a glowing coal at one end, while the other end was cool enough to hold. The coal made a dim point of light which tarnished quickly in the open air, and then freshened to an amazing degree when blown upon.

Standing Bull was satisfied. It would have been very well if he could have guessed in what room the girl was sleeping, but since he did not know, he would have to look.

All the doors stood open upon the big kitchen, in order that the fire might send its heat through all the chambers. This was partly an advantage and partly a great disaster. For though it meant that he would have no difficulty in opening the doors, yet every move that he made was now likely to strike upon the ears of all the sleepers.

The two helpers went behind him. He had told them beforehand what he wanted them to do. He dared not intrust the actual kidnaping to them. He felt that the body of this slender white girl was so fragile that it would have to be touched with the greatest care.

He stepped through the first doorway. It was like walking into the throat of a cannon. Then, blowing softly on the dying coal, he got from it the faintest of glows, yet enough to enable his straining eyes to distinguish the vast shoulders of the white hunter in the bed.

Instantly he veiled the coal with his hand, and as he stepped back toward the door, he was startled to hear a woman's voice exclaim: "Sam! Oh, Sam!"

"Aye?" growled big Samuel Brett.

"There's something wrong!"

"What could be wrong?"

"I—I don't know—I just have a feeling. Sam, do get up and see if everything's all right!"

"Now, what's ailin' you?" asked Samuel Brett. "What could be wrong?"

The Indian, in the darkness by the door, kept his hand on the haft of his knife. What the words meant, he could not understand. But his very blood was frozen with fear.

"I dunno—"

"I *do* know. Nobody could get past that dog. It's got eight legs and two heads. It can look both ways at once. I never seen such a dog! And if it found a man, it'd eat him!"

"Suppose that he was knocked senseless—"

"Supposin' that the sky wasn't blue, well, it might be green!"

"You can bully all you please. I tell you, I got a feelin' that there's somebody in this house!"

"Hey? What?" asked Samuel Brett in changed tones. "Well, I'll get up and look around."

The bed squeaked as he sat up. But then the cool of the night air made him shiver.

"I'm darned if I get up and catch a cold for the sake of pleasin' the whim of a silly old woman. You go to sleep and leave me be!"

He settled back with a groan of comfort into the warmness of the bed. In the meantime, freed from the direct danger, Standing Bull drew once more into the kitchen.

There were two other doorways. Into which one should he go next?

He chose the middle one. A gesture in the dark placed both the Cheyennes on guard at the door of the white man's room. Then Standing Bull proceeded into the next chamber. At the first flare of the coal beneath his breath he found himself looking into the same face which he had seen in the kitchen of the house—the same pale face, the same pale hair. But the eyes were not dim. They were sparkling and wide with incalculable terror as the girl sat up in the bed and supported herself with both shaking arms.

How long had she been there, awake, listening, thinking that she heard a sound, denying that it could be so!

Standing Bull went straight toward her and she shrank back against the wall. Her lips parted and her throat worked, but no scream would come.

Time was short with Standing Bull and every instant in that house was of infinite danger to him; yet he dared not take her out into such a night clad only in a thin nightgown of cheap cotton.

He pointed to the clothes which lay upon a chair and made a commanding gesture. She obeyed, her enchanted eyes of terror fixed on him, and her movements slow, like those of one whose body is numbed with deadly cold.

He had drawn a knife that the fear of it might stimulate her and keep her from screaming for help. Under the dull glow of the coal, the blade of that knife seemed to run again with blood, and he could see her like a shadow among shadows dressing with stumbling hands and numb fingers from which the clothes slipped away.

At last, at a sound in the next room, he could wait no longer. He caught up a heavy buffalo robe which covered the foot of the bed, and throwing it around Nancy Brett, took her in his arms. Hers was like the weight of a child, thought Standing Bull. He strode to the door of the chamber. Inside the next room, Samuel Brett was rumbling: "Darn me if I can go to sleep. Where did you leave the candle? Eh?"

There was a noise of fumbling. The man of the house began to mutter beneath his breath, impatiently. But Standing Bull with his burden went on toward the rear door, and with Rushing Wind carefully opening it, he passed through and out into the night.

There had been only one sound from his captive, and that, as they reached the open air, was a faint sigh. She became limp in his arms and he knew that she had fainted.

So much the better!

He began to run. Inside the house there was a sudden shout. The rear door was slammed shut with a great crash, as Red Shirt leaped through and swung the door to behind him. In another moment the whole settlement would be up.

CHAPTER XV

★

Escape

The shout of Samuel Brett was enough to have alarmed whole legions. And the ears to which that shout did not reach certainly were touched by the sound of rifle shots, as Brett ran from his house toward his horses. From every house men began to turn out, but for a time they were a little uncertain as to whether they should fly to the fort for protection, stand firm on the defense, or else act as aggressors.

In the meantime, Standing Bull had reached his horses. He mounted. It was unfortunate that the girl had to be carried. But perhaps it was better to have her senseless than that with her screams she should guide the whites as with a flaming torch.

The five galloped back to the main body of the horses at the edge of the wood—the whole body then rushed out across the plain beyond, and the thick curtain of the rain drew together instantly behind them.

The care with which Standing Bull had distributed his forces for the start now began to tell, for there was no sign of sudden pursuit. He did not follow the river, but cut back across the hill, hoping that the enemy would hunt for the Cheyennes along the river banks, for that was the easiest course. In that direction the greatest number of miles could be made.

Now, when the first rush of the flight was over, Nancy Brett recovered her senses with a groan. She was given no sympathy. They made the briefest of halts, during which she was clapped into a saddle and tied securely to it. A whip cracked on the haunches of the half-wild Indian pony. It pitched high into the air, and came down running, with the Indians rushing their own mounts beside it. So they dashed on into the night, and the cold whip of the rain in her face began to rouse Nancy Brett.

It was so strange, so utterly incomprehensible, that her mind was in a whirl. She knew something about Indians and their ways. They might capture the daughter of a great and rich man and hold her for ransom. Or an Indian might even kidnap a woman with whom he was in love. But she was certain that neither of these motives appeared here.

She was sure that she never had seen this monster of an Indian before. And as they tore on through the night and the dawn began to come nearer, she looked more curiously at her captor. No, she never had seen that homely profile before.

When day came, they pitched camp—or rather made a short halt—at the bank of a stream. There the saddles were changed, the used horses turned into the herd, and the next best mounts requisitioned. In this way, they would shift the saddles half a dozen times in twenty-four hours of work, reusing the horses in turn. Standing Bull, regarding his captive, was amazed to find that she seemed to be bearing up against fatigue and fear very well indeed. There was more color in her face than there had been when she wept in the kitchen of the house of Samuel Brett.

He wished that he possessed sufficient English to pronounce the name of the great white medicine man to whom he was bringing her. But he did not even know that name in the first place.

She made no trouble, however. Her grave, blue eyes never stared at them. She seemed only watchful to do what was wanted of her. And Standing Bull wondered greatly! She acted, in fact, almost as an Indian girl would have acted at such a time as this!

All the day they rode on under a gray sky. There were only the halts for the changing of saddles, and to eat a little dried meat at the same time. The girl was no longer tied to her horse, but the pony she rode was tethered to the saddle of Standing Bull. He watched her begin to droop as the afternoon wore away. When they at last halted on the edge of night, she almost fell from the saddle.

"She must sleep," said Red Shirt uneasily, and looked toward the northwestern horizon.

"She must sleep," answered Standing Bull. "But first she must eat!"

She would have refused food. He commanded with a savage growl, and she choked down a few morsels in fear. Then, wrapped in a robe, she slept. The Indians already were sleeping, except Standing Bull. He needed no sleep. His heart was full of glory for the thing which he had done. He began to frame in his mind the song he would sing when he reappeared in the Cheyenne village. The notes of the chant ached in his throat and the sweetness of fame among his fellows made the head of Standing Bull sway a little from side to side.

The sky cleared during the night. When the clouds had blown down to the horizon, he roused his sleepy command. He touched the girl, and she sprang to her feet with a faint cry. In two minutes they were on their way again.

So they pressed on until they were three days from Fort Kendry, and trouble for the first time overtook them. Had it not been for Nancy Brett, they could have made somewhat better time, and yet the horses hardly could have stood up to more work. They were growing very thin. Sometimes at a halt many of them were too weary to begin to graze.

And while the party was in this condition, on the pale verge of morning, saddling for the day's ride, Yellow Man was seen to throw up his hands, whirl, and fall without sound, while the sharp, small clang of a rifle struck at their ears. Glancing wildly about them, they could see a wisp of smoke rising above a small cluster of shrubs and trees near by.

"Take two men," said Standing Bull to Red Shirt. "Take three if you will, and go back. If there is one man, bring us his scalp. It there are more, skirmish and delay them!"

Red Shirt went instantly to execute the order. With Standing Bull and the girl remained only that capable young brave, Rushing Wind. And the three of them with the larger body of the horses struck away across the prairie.

As they did so, they saw Red Shirt's party approach the trees in a wide circle, and out from the trees rode a man on a fine, gray horse.

Roger Lincoln!

They knew well that it was he the instant the gray began to run. It was not likely that two gray horses on that prairie had the long and flowing gallop of the mare, Comanche! She drifted easily away toward the north, with the party of Red Shirt and his three braves hopelessly laboring in the rear.

Glancing keenly at the girl, Standing Bull made sure by the light in her eye that she, too, had recognized the rescuer and that hope had come to her. So strong was that hope that it enabled her to endure a whole day of savage riding, and as the evening drew near they knew that the Cheyenne village was not far away. So great had their speed been that the party sent back to block Roger Lincoln had not been sighted again since first they disappeared. Perhaps the gray mare had failed, after all, and the four warriors now were blockading Roger Lincoln in some nest of rocks!

So hoped Standing Bull, and smiled at the thought. He talked with Rushing Wind as they changed saddles for the last time. Yellow Man had fulfilled his weird dream of the night before. He was dead, but his body, lashed to a pony's back, was being brought back to his family. Not two hours of steady riding lay before them.

And if the girl collapsed, they could tie her to her saddle and finish the ride at any rate, like a whirlwind covering the plains.

So, as they made the change of saddles, they helped her to her new mount. She was a dead weight in their hands. With sunken head and lips compressed, she sat the saddle, both hands clinging feebly to the pommel.

"Tie her now in her place," suggested Rushing Wind. "She is very weak."

It was done at once, and while Standing Bull made sure that the fastenings were secure, he heard an excited call from Rushing Wind.

On the northern horizon, clearly seen against the red of the sunset sky, there was a flash as of silver, and when Standing Bull looked more closely he made out a horseman coming steadily toward them.

Roger Lincoln! Or was it one of the Cheyennes who, having killed Lincoln, had sent back one of their number on the captured horse to give the news to the village and bring out food and a doctor to the wounded of the party?

So muttered Standing Bull, but Rushing Wind cried excitedly: "I tell you I can see that it is the white man. I can see the paleness of his long hair about his shoulders even at this distance. But what has become of the others?"

"He has dodged them," said Standing Bull gloomily. "Or else—"

"Or else he has killed them!" exclaimed Rushing Wind. "He has killed them, Standing Bull. I feel that they are dead men and that we never shall look on them again. Shall we go back to face him?"

"He has great medicine in his rifle," said Standing Bull in grave thought, "but I would not run away from any single warrior. Nevertheless, it is not for us to think of ourselves. We are working to bring happiness to White Thunder, and through him to the entire tribe. Is it true?"

"That is true," admitted the boy, still staring at the far distant rider.

"Let us finish that work. Afterward we may be able to ride out and find Roger Lincoln on the war trail. I hope so! In his death there would be enough fame to make ten braves happy. Now let us ride. Pray to the wind to help on our horses, or the white man will send our souls where he has sent all five of our companions before us! Ride, Rushing Wind, and call on the ghosts of our fathers to make the legs of our horses strong!"

By the time they were in the saddle, the form of Roger Lincoln was beginning to grow more and more distinct until, even in that half light, they were sure of the blond hair about his shoulders.

Nancy Brett cast one last, desperate look over her shoulder, and then set her teeth to endure the last stage of the journey as well as she could. If she was not strong, she was not brittle stuff that breaks. Only by degrees her power had failed her in this long forced march. Making no effort to keep the horse herd running before them now, Standing Bull drove the last three ponies straight across the prairie and toward the Cheyenne village.

CHAPTER XVI

★

Journey's End

How earnestly Standing Bull prayed for the night, then! And night was coming down upon them fast. In a few moments, there would not be sufficient illumination to enable the white man to use the great magic of his rifle on the Cheyennes, and without that gun Standing Bull feared Lincoln not at all.

But the gray mare, Comanche, drew closer and closer. She seemed supported on wings, so rapidly did she overtake the straining Indian ponies.

She had been matching her wonderful speed that day against half a dozen animals, and yet she had the strength to make such a final burst as this! Standing Bull, throwing glances over his shoulder from moment to moment, suddenly exclaimed: "Rushing Wind, my brother! Look and tell me if what I think is true! That the gray gains on us no longer!"

Back came the joyous cry of the younger brave: "She has lost her wings. She is flying no longer!"

"Ride hard, ride hard!" urged Standing Bull. "Now that he cannot gain, he will no longer try to push the mare. He will take to the ground and fire on us."

He had rightly interpreted the intention of the white scout. Now that the last strength had gone from beautiful Comanche, Roger Lincoln pulled her up short and dropped to his full length on the prairie. It was wonderfully long range, and the light was very bad indeed—far less than a half light! Yet at the explosion of the gun, Rushing Wind ducked his head and lurched forward with a stifled cry.

"Brother, brother!" called Standing Bull anxiously. "Did the bullet strike you?"

"No, no!" answered the boy. "But I heard it singing past me more loudly than a hornet. I am not hurt. Heammawihio, to you I vow a fine buffalo hide, well painted. I shall make your heart glad because you have saved me to-day."

There was no second report. In another moment they were out of sight of Roger Lincoln in the thickening dust. And now the stars began to come out, pale and winking. Other lights like stars, like red stars, appeared on the southern horizon.

"That is our city," said Standing Bull. "We are free from pursuit."

He drew up his horse. So weak was the girl that, as her horse stopped, she lurched forward and almost sprawled to the ground. But she recovered at once, and stood with stiffened lip.

"Look!" said Standing Bull to his fellow warrior. "I have never seen such a woman before. I saw her in the house in Fort Kendry, crying as a baby cries. So, so! I smiled and thought she was worthless. But you see, my friend! Out of such metal a man could make arrow heads and knives. White Thunder—you will see! He will be mad with joy!"

"I shall stand by and watch," said Rushing Wind, laughing. "He pretends that nothing matters to him. He yawns when warriors make great gifts to him. But now we will see him cry out and shout and dance. But, for me, I prefer the girls of the Cheyennes. It needs a strong back to dig roots and a big hand to hold an ax."

Standing Bull, however, made no answer. Once or twice he turned and stared earnestly into the darkness behind him, but there was no sound or trace of Roger Lincoln. It was as though he had permitted the night to swallow him after that single shot into which he had thrown all his skill.

Now the Indian leader rode close to the girl. With a strong hand beneath her arm, he supported her greatly. She let her head fall straight back, sometimes, so utterly weakened was she.

"She is tired. She is like a dead reed. It may break in the wind, Standing Bull," cautioned the younger man.

And again Standing Bull made no reply, but looked earnestly on the face of the girl. There was no moon. There were no stars. Yet he could see her. It was as though he beheld her by the light of her own whiteness.

They came to the edge of the village before they were discovered. They entered, of course, in the midst of pandemonium. And straight they went to the lodge of White Thunder. It was as white as his name, made of the skins of nineteen buffalo cows, all of an age, all killed at the perfect season, or cured in exactly the same fashion.

Fires glimmered dimly through open lodge entrances. In the center of White Thunder's lodge there was a fire also. Standing Bull took the girl from her horse. She lay in his arms with closed eyes.

Then he stalked into the lodge.

Paul Torridon lolled against a back rest by the firelight, carefully sharpening a knife. Young Willow was at work cleaning the great iron cooking pot which simmered over the central fire all the day.

"Brother," said Standing Bull, "I have come back from a far land and a far people to bring you a present."

At the sound of his voice, all the noise outside the lodge was hushed. Only a child cried out, and the slap of a rebuking hand sounded like the popping of a whiplash. All that Standing Bull said clearly could be heard.

"When I brought you alone," said Standing Bull simply, "I saw that you were unhappy. I decided that I would bring you a present that would fill your lodge with content."

Here Torridon stood up and waved a hand in acknowledgment. Then, taking closer heed to the burden which the big Indian carried in his arms, Torridon stepped closer.

"She should be worth much to you," said Standing Bull in conclusion, "because five good men and brave warriors have died that she might be brought to you."

Suddenly he stretched out his arms and the burden in them. Torridon peered at it curiously, the white face, the closed eyes—and then with a great cry he caught Nancy Brett to his breast. Young Willow, her eyes glittering like polished steel, threw a robe beside the fire, and on it Torridon kneeled, and then laid down the girl, crying out her name in a voice half of joy and half of sorrow.

Standing Bull strode from the tepee, herding Rushing Wind before him into the outer darkness.

He raised his great arm and stilled the clamor which began to break out from the crowd that surrounded him.

"Be still," said he. "In that lodge there is a woman who is worth five men. Heammawihio demanded their lives before we could bring her here. And he knows the worth of human beings. It is her spirit that is great. Her body is not strong. Now all go away. Your shouting would kill her. Go away. The village should be silent."

Out of respect for him, the throng was still. He walked through them to his tepee, and there was Owl Woman, the perfect wife, waiting to greet him. The firelight turned her to golden copper; her smile was beautiful. But to Standing Bull she suddenly seemed like a hideous cartoon of a woman, with a vast, stretching mouth, and a great nose, and high cheek bones. He made himself take her in his arms. She had been boiling fat meat in the pot. The odor of cookery clung to her garments. And Standing Bull remembered how he had ridden grandly from Fort Kendry, and the slender body which had lain in his arms, and the fragrance as of spring wild flowers which had blown from her hair against his face.

PART TWO

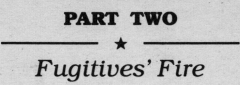

Fugitives' Fire

CHAPTER XVII

★

A Lying Dream

It was a small band of buffalo, an offscouring or little side eddy from one of the black masses of millions which moved across the plains, and when Rushing Wind came on their traces his heart leaped with the lust for fresh meat. Parched corn and dried buffalo flesh, tasteless as dry chips of wood, had been his diet for days during a lonely excursion upon the prairie. He had gone out from the Cheyenne village like some knight of the olden days, riding aimlessly, praying for adventure, hoping greedily for scalps and for coups to be counted. But no fortune had come his way. For ten days, patient as a hungry wolf, he had dogged the way of a caravan of white men, pushing west and west, but he had had no luck. In the night they guarded their circle of wagons with the most scrupulous care. In the day, their hunting parties were never less than three well-armed men. And though their plainscraft might not be of a very high order, it was an old maxim among the Cheyennes that all white men shoot straight with a rifle. The Indians were apt to attribute it to bigger medicine. As a matter of fact, it was simply that the whites had infinitely more powder and ball to use in practice. The red man had to get his practice out of actual hunting or battle. Accordingly, Rushing Wind had at last turned off from the way of the caravan and struck at a tangent from its line across the prairie, and now he had come upon the trail of the buffalo.

When he first came on the trail, he leaned from the saddle and studied the prints. The grass was beginning to curl up and straighten again around the marks of the hoofs. So he knew that the animals had passed within a few hours. He set off after them cautiously, creeping up to the top of every swale of ground.

It was a typical plains day; bright, warm, and so crystal-clear that the horizon line seemed ruled in ink. Presently he saw the moving forms far off. They were drifting and grazing to the south. The wind lay in the southeast. Therefore, he threw a long, loose circle to the north and west, coming up cautiously in the shelter of some slightly rising ground.

Coming to the crest, he dismounted, and lay flat in the tall grass. This he parted before his face and looked out. He was very close to them. There was a magnificent bull. He admired the huge front, the lofty shoulders of the animal, but he knew that the flesh of such an experienced monster would be rank to the taste and so tough that teeth hardly could manage it—not even such white, strong teeth as armed the mouth of this Cheyenne. Then he slid backward through the grass.

As he did so, a second rider to the rear, a man on a silver-flashing, gray mare, dismounted and sank into the grass, and his horse sank down with him.

Rushing Wind sat up and looked all round him, as though some shadow of danger had swept across his mind, like the dark of a cloud across the ground. It was not fear of immediate danger, however. It was merely the usual caution of a wild thing hunting in the wilderness, and, therefore, in constant dread of being hunted. For just as he had wandered across the plains in search of adventure and scalps and coups and plunder, so many another individual was cruising about the prairies, as keen as he, as crafty, as clever with weapons, as merciless.

Seeing nothing between him and the horizon, however, the young Cheyenne returned to his patient horse and took from the case strapped behind his saddle a strong war bow made of the toughest horn of the mountain sheep, boiled, straightened, and then blued and bound together in strips. It was flexible enough to stand infinite bending and yet stiff enough to require all the weight of a strong man's shoulder to draw an arrow home against such resistance.

He had a long and heavy rifle as well but, as usual, he was

abroad with a most scanty supply of the precious powder and lead. He had to save that for human enemies. He strung the bow with some difficulty, tried the strength of the beautifully made cord by drawing it to his shoulder several times, and then selected from the quiver several hunting arrows—that is arrows which having been shot into game could be drawn forth, and the head, at least, used again and again. The arrows for war, of which he had an additional small supply, were barbed so that it would be a murderous task to draw them from the flesh.

When he had made sure that the bow was in good condition and the arrows all that he desired, he planted in the ground his long lance, hung his shield upon it, with the festoon of eagle feathers hanging from its face, and then carefully leaned the invaluable rifle against this stand. Next he loosed the packs from behind the saddle of the pony.

It might be that the chase would be long. In any case, the pony needed all its agility in the dangerous task that lay before it. After that, he stood before the head of the horse and looked keenly into its eyes.

They were like the eyes of a beast of prey—bright, treacherous, wild. But the Indian looked for no softness and kindness there. He would have been suspicious of a friendly glance. What he wanted was what he found—untamable fierceness, endurance, force of heart.

Assured of this, he bounded into the saddle and began to work the pony around the edge of the hill with much caution, for the buffalo sometimes seemed to be endowed with an extra sense which told them of approaching danger.

In fact, as he rounded the hill, he saw the entire little herd rushing off at full speed, their hoofs clacking sharply together, the ground trembling under the beat of their heavy striding.

He was after them with a yell. Heavy and cumbersome as the buffalo looks, he can run at a good pace, and he can maintain it through a wonderful length of time. It takes a good horse to come up with them, but the pony which this young brave bestrode was the best of his herd, and his own herd was a hand-picked lot.

Like an antelope it flashed forward. It passed a lumbering

yearling. It ranged beside a three-year-old cow. Then the bow was at work at once. Drawn to the shoulder, it drove a shaft with wonderful force. At four hundred yards a Cheyenne bow had been known to strike game and to kill it. And if Rushing Wind was an archer not quite up to such a mark as this, at least, he sent the shaft into the side of the cow behind the shoulder almost up to the feathers.

The big animal swerved, coughed, and then dropped upon its knees, skidding forward through the grass.

That was food for the Cheyenne. His sport was still ahead of him, and with a yell he sent the pony forward. The bull ran well, but there was still a burst of sprinting left in the horse. It carried its master straight up to the panting bull, and a second arrow went from the bow.

This time it struck dense bull hide. It sank deep in the flesh of the big fellow, but the roll of muscles and the looseness of the skin itself forced the arrow upward. The bull was merely stung, and he whirled toward the rider with such suddenness that the second arrow that flew from the string merely ripped a furrow in the tough back of the buffalo.

With a roar came the bull, a veteran of many a battle with his kind and ready to fight once more against such a strange foe. The surge of its head swept past the flank of the pony narrowly as the active little horse bounded to the side.

Presenting his battle front, circling as the Indian circled, the bull waited, tearing up the ground, sending his long, strange bellow booming, so that it seemed to be flooding up from the earth itself and rising now here, now there.

Rushing Wind, his eyes on fire, began to maneuver the little pony like a dancer, but it was some moments before the foaming horse made the bull make a false step that left the tender flank open again. Then loudly twanged the bow string, and the arrow sank into the side of the monster half the length of the shaft.

The bull charged, but blindly. He came to a halt, tossing his head. His hide twitched convulsively, so that the two arrows imbedded in him jerked back and forth. His head lowered. Blood burst from his mouth. He sank to his knees, and even then, with more courage than strength, he strove to rise, and still he boomed his defiance. Life was passing from him quickly, however. Before the last of his fleeing herd was out of sight, he rolled upon his side, dead.

From the carcass, the Cheyenne took only the tongue. He returned to the cow, took from her the tongue also, and then prepared to remove some other choice bits. He would gorge himself in a great feast, dry the flesh that remained in strips, and then set himself for the homeward journey. It was not a great thing to have killed two buffalo, but it was better than nothing, and it was, perhaps, the explanation of the dream which had sent him forth to try his fortune in the open country alone. At least, he had not so much as broken the shaft of an arrow in this encounter. The arrows, soon cleaned and restored to his quiver, were as good as ever, though they might be the better for a little sharpening.

On the whole, the heart of Rushing Wind was high, and he returned cheerfully to the point where he had left his other weapons, hastening a little on his still sweating horse, because he was as anxious about the welfare of the rifle as though it were a favorite child.

He sighed with relief when he found that lance and shield and rifle and pack were all in place, and, dismounting, he looked first to the gun, stroking it with a smile. It was half weapon and half "medicine," in the eyes of Rushing Wind. He had only one thing more precious, and that was the richly ornamented hunting knife in his belt, the gift of that prince of doctors and medicine men, White Thunder.

Something stirred just behind the Indian. It was no more than the slightest of whispers in the grass, but it made the young Cheyenne twist sharply around.

He found a white hunter risen to his knees in the grass, a long rifle at his shoulder, and a deadly aim taken upon his own heart.

"Stand fast," said the white man. "Drop your rifle. You still may live to return to your lodge."

He spoke in fairly good Cheyenne, and the young brave said with a groan: "Roger Lincoln!" Clumsily the English words came upon his tongue. "And the dream was a lying dream that was sent to me!"

CHAPTER XVIII

★

The Talk of Friends

In the first place, Rushing Wind was disarmed. Some brush grew near by, hardly ankle high. Then, at the suggestion of the white man, they gathered some of this brush. They made a fire and began to roast bits of the tender buffalo tongues on the ends of twigs. While they cooked, they talked, the Cheyenne with a rising heart.

Roger Lincoln said in the beginning: "You were with Standing Bull when he came to Fort Kendry and first stole away Paul Torridon, whom you call White Thunder?"

"I was not," said the Cheyenne.

"But you were with Standing Bull when he came up again and captured the white girl, Nancy Brett, and took her away across the plains?"

The young Indian raised his head and was silent. His eyes grew a little larger, as though he were in expectation of an outburst of enmity. But Roger Lincoln pointed to the little fire which was burning so cheerfully.

"We are cooking food together. When we eat together we are friends, Rushing Wind, are we not?"

The other hesitated.

"It was I who was with Standing Bull," he said. "Why should I deny it? You saw me with him. I was with him when you offered all the guns and horses if he would set White Thunder free."

"But you would not do that."

"How could Standing Bull promise? How could any of us promise? Not even High Wolf, the greatest of our chiefs, could send him away. The people would not endure to see him go. They know what he has done for us!"

Roger Lincoln nodded and frowned.

"He has made rain for you, and through him you've killed a good many Dakotas."

"And he has healed the sick and given good luck to the men on the warpath. He brings the buffalo to the side of the village!" added Rushing Wind.

"Those things have happened now and then. He doesn't do them every day."

"A man cannot hope to take scalps every day of his life," said Rushing Wind naïvely. "And," he added, growing more sad, "I never have taken a single one!"

"All is in the hands of Heammawihio," said the white man. "All that a warrior can do is to be brave and ready. Heammawihio sends the good fortune and the bad! Tell me, are you a friend of White Thunder in the camp?"

The eye of the youth brightened. He took from his belt the hunting knife with the gaudy handle. Roger Lincoln had not troubled to remove that means of attack from his captive; as though he knew that his own great name and fame would be sufficient to keep the youngster from attacking hand to hand.

"This," said the young Cheyenne, "was given to me by White Thunder. You may judge if he is my friend!"

"And Standing Bull. He also is your friend?"

"He is a friend to White Thunder. Not to me. Standing Bull," went on the boy carefully, "is a great chief!" He explained still further: "White Thunder has made him great!"

"No," said Lincoln. "Any man who dared to come into the middle of Fort Kendry twice and steal away whites is great without any help. But although this man is a great chief, he is not a great friend of yours?"

The boy was silent.

"Very well," said Roger Lincoln. "We cannot be friends with every one. That isn't to be expected. But now I want you to look at everything with my eyes."

"I shall try," said the boy. "You are a great hunter of bears and buffalo—and men."

He let his brow darken a little as he said this.

"Tell me," said Roger Lincoln. "Before White Thunder was stolen away, was I not a friend to the Cheyennes?"

"It is true," said the boy.

"He is my best of companions and friends," said Roger Lincoln. "Once my life lay at his feet like this fire at ours. He could have let it be stamped out, but he would not do that. He saved my life. And at that time I was a stranger to him. I was large and he was small. I was strong and he was weak. Now, after he had done that much for me, I ask you to tell me if he should not be my friend?"

The Cheyenne listened to this story with glistening eyes.

"It is true," he said, and his harsh voice became soft and pleasant.

"However, he was stolen away by Standing Bull, whose life also White Thunder had saved," continued Roger Lincoln.

"Yes," said Rushing Wind, "and more than his life, his spirit."

"And after he was taken away, what should I do? Should I sit in my lodge and fold my hands?"

"No," replied Rushing Wind carefully. "You should have put on the war paint and gone on the warpath. And you have done it," he added. A glitter came in his eyes. "Six Cheyennes have died. Their names are gone. Their souls have rotted with their bodies on the prairies!"

He looked keenly at Roger Lincoln.

"I am the seventh man," said he.

"You are not," replied the great hunter. "We eat together side by side. I give you my friendship."

Rushing Wind replied, still hesitant: "The hawk and the eagle never fly side by side."

"Listen to me, hear with my ears and believe with my mind. In my day I have killed warriors. The list of them is not short. It would be a small pleasure to me to add one more man to the number who have gone stumbling before me to the house of darkness. But you can do a great service to me out of good will and with your life still yours!"

The Cheyenne was silent, but obviously he was listening with all his might to this novel suggestion.

"I cannot buy your good will," said Roger Lincoln, "but I give your life back to you as a peace offering. This thing I will do, and I promise that I shall not take my gift back. Besides this, I ask no promise in return from you. I shall tell you the thing which I wish to do. Afterward, you will think. Perhaps you will wish to do what I want. Perhaps you will merely smile and laugh to yourself and say that I have talked like a fool."

He made a pause and began to eat heartily of the roasted tongue. The Cheyenne imitated that good example, and though he was a smaller man by far than Roger Lincoln, and though the white man had fasted the longer of the two, yet the Indian fairly ate two pounds for the one of his captor.

At last, Roger Lincoln pushed back a little from the fire. He filled a short-stemmed pipe and began to smoke strong tobacco. The Indian, however, took out a bowl of red catlinite, which he filled with a mixture, always holding the stem up as he worked. Then he lighted the tobacco and flavoring herbs with a coal from the little dying fire and began to smoke, after first blowing, as it were, libations to the spirit world.

Neither of them spoke until after a few minutes. Then Roger Lincoln said: "How did the girl come to the village?"

"She was very tired."

"Was she taken to the tepee of White Thunder?"

"Yes."

"How did he receive her?"

"In his arms. He—"

The Cheyenne paused. And Roger Lincoln was silent, frowning with a desperate blackness at the sky before him.

"He received her also," said Rushing Wind, "with tears."

His face was actually puckered with emotion as he said this. Plainly he could hardly connect the word "tears" with the word "man" and control his disgust. A flicker of contempt went over the face of Roger Lincoln also. Men told their stories of how Roger Lincoln, on a time, had been tormented almost to death by a party of Crows, and how he had laughed at them and reviled them with scorn, heedless of his pain, until he was rescued by the luckiest of chances. So, being such a man as he was, he could not help that touch of scorn appearing in his face.

However, he came instantly to the defense of his absent friend. "No man can have all the strength in the world," said he.

"It is true," said the Cheyenne earnestly. "I would not have White Thunder think that I have spoken with scorn about him."

He glanced upward with awe and trouble in his face, as though he feared that a circling buzzard far above them might be an emissary sent by the medicine man to spy upon his words.

"However," said the Cheyenne, "everything is as I have told you. She began to wake up and hold out her arms to him. She was tired but happy."

"So!" said the hunter.

He kept silence, being deep in thought. At last he went on in a changed and gruffer voice: "He took her into his tepee?"

"Yes."

"He has kept her there ever since?"

"Yes."

Roger Lincoln exclaimed with something between disgust, impatience and anger: "Then he has taken her as his wife, as an Indian takes a wife?"

At this, the Cheyenne shook his head.

"Who is to understand the ways of people who are guided by the spirits and the Sky People?" said he naïvely. "I, at least, cannot understand them!"

"Why do you say that?"

"It is a big lodge," said the young warrior. "There is no whiter or finer lodge in all the camp of the Cheyennes. And now one part of it is walled off with curtains of deer skin from another part. And when they sleep, the girl goes into one side as though it were a separate lodge, and White Thunder goes into another part."

The light reappeared in the eye of Roger Lincoln.

"A good lad!" he exclaimed. "I had written him down a good lad! I would have wagered my blood on him!"

"Ha?" grunted Rushing Wind. "Then is this a mystery which you, also, understand?"

CHAPTER XIX

★

The Power of White Thunder

They stared for a moment at one another. But, since it was not the first time in the life of either that he had been aware of the great difference and distinction between the viewpoint of red man and white, they passed on in their conversation, Roger Lincoln taking the lead.

"The girl is now happy?" he asked. "Or does she sit and weep?"

"Weep?" said the Indian. "Why should a woman weep when she has become the squaw of a great medicine man such as White Thunder? No, she is singing and laughing all day long!"

The white man smiled a little.

"Besides," said the Cheyenne, "she does little work. Her hands are not as big as my two fingers. Young Willow still keeps the lodge for White Thunder!"

"And what of White Thunder himself? Is he happy, also?"

"He is more happy than he was," said the boy. "He is able to ride out now on the great, black horse."

"Is he free, then?"

"Yes. He is not guarded except when the girl rides out with him, also. But when she is left behind in the lodge, the chiefs know that he will not go far."

"How far does he go?"

"Sometimes he is gone in the morning and when he comes back in the evening even the black horse is tired."

"There is no other horse like that one," admitted Roger

Lincoln. "Though there was a time when I thought that Comanche was the swiftest foot on the prairie!"

He pointed to her and she, hearing her name and marking the gesture, came forward fearlessly, gently, toward her master.

"It is plain that White Thunder put a spirit in her when he had her," said Rushing Wind. "She, also, understands man talk, as the black horse does!"

"Does the black horse understand man talk?" queried Roger Lincoln, suppressing a smile.

"Perfectly," said the Cheyenne in all seriousness. "So well does the stallion understand, that he repeated to his master what the herd boys said to one another when they were out watching the horse!"

He began to fill his pipe again, observing the same careful formula as before.

"Ah, then," said Roger Lincoln, "people must be careful of what they say in front of this clever horse!"

"As much so," replied the Cheyenne, "as if it were his master that listened. The tall brave with the scarred face, Walking Horse, said when he was near the big stallion that he thought White Thunder was a coward and not a good man. Not a week later Walking Horse's son fell sick and would have died. But Walking Horse took the boy and went to the lodge of White Thunder. He confessed his fault and asked for pardon, and begged White Thunder not to take away the life of his boy. So White Thunder kept the boy in his own lodge and made big medicine, and in a few days the boy could run home. Then Walking Horse gave White Thunder many good robes, and ten fine horses from his herd!"

"By this I see," said Roger Lincoln, "that my good friend White Thunder is growing rich!"

"He would be," replied the young brave, "the richest man who ever walked or rode among the Cheyennes. But what is wealth to him? It runs through his fingers. He gives to the poor of the tribe. He mounts the poor warriors from his horse herd and lets them keep the horses. His lodge is open to the hungry. What is wealth to him! He can ask more from the Sky People if there should be need!"

This speech he made with perfect simplicity and openness of manner, and Roger Lincoln, watching narrowly, nodded his head.

"But still White Thunder is not happy?" said he.

"It is true that often he looks toward the horizon," was the answer.

"Then let me speak the truth. Has this medicine man great power?"

"That we all have seen."

"Has he struck down even the Dakotas with his wisdom?"

"And they turn aside, now, from our war trails," said the youth with a smile of savage triumph. "They are familiar with the medicine of White Thunder, and they do not wish to anger him again! They have not tried to strike us since the last battle. Even Spotted Antelope cannot find braves to follow him south against our lodges. They know that the birds of White Thunder would watch them coming."

"Do the birds work for White Thunder, then?"

"Yes. Do you see that buzzard still hanging in the sky above us?"

"Perhaps he is waiting until we go, so that he can drop down on the dead buffalo, yonder?"

"Perhaps," said the boy, but his smile showed that he was confident in his superior knowledge.

"Further," he expanded suddenly, "than they can smell dead meat, the buzzards and all the other birds can hear the name of White Thunder, and they come to listen, and to talk to him."

"It is a great power," said Roger Lincoln, keeping a grave face.

"I myself," said the youth, "have seen a sparrow fly out from the lodge entrance of White Thunder!"

Roger Lincoln, after this crushing proof, remained respectfully silent for some time.

"Now tell me," said he, "if he has this great power, and if he is not happy among the Cheyennes, what keeps him from one day striking a great blow against the Cheyennes?"

"We are his people," said the boy uneasily. "He was sent to us! Standing Bull brought him!"

"Did not White Thunder once ride away from you?"

"That is true," admitted the Cheyenne.

"May not White Thunder be waiting patiently, hoping that because of the great services he has rendered to your people they will soon set him free, and let him go, with many horses to carry him and his possessions over the prairie?"

The young warrior was silent, scowling at the thought.

"And when he finds that the thing is not done, may he not lose his patience, at last? May he not strike down the whole village with sickness, and while they die, he will ride away?"

Rushing Wind opened his eyes very wide.

And, striking while the iron was hot, Roger Lincoln continued: "Now I shall tell you why my rifle did not strike you to-day. A dream came to me. My friend, White Thunder, stood before me and said: 'Every day I say to High Wolf and the other Cheyennes that I wish to be gone. They will not listen. Therefore, come and tell them for me. They may believe you. They are like children. They do not think that I shall strike them. Tell them. They may believe your tongue when they will not believe mine!'"

He paused, and Rushing Wind sat tense with fear and excitement.

"If I live to reach the village, I shall carry the word to High Wolf," said he.

"That would be the act of a very young man," said Roger Lincoln.

"What should I do?"

"If you tell the chiefs, they will sit and do a great deal of talking with the old men. Everybody will talk."

"That is true," nodded the young warrior. "A great many words—many feasts—and nothing is done!"

"At last they will not be able to give up White Thunder. He is precious to them. A man does not like to sacrifice his best rifle!"

"True!" said the Cheyenne again, wincing as he let his gaze rest upon his beloved weapon.

"And White Thunder is like a rifle to the Cheyennes!"

"Then what should I do?"

"Be a brave and bold man, for your own sake, for your friendship to White Thunder, for the sake of your whole tribe—

and for the sake, perhaps, of the life which I have given back to you this day!"

Rushing Wind listened to this solemn prologue with grave, bright eyes.

"The day will soon come when you will be a guard with White Thunder in your care."

"True," said the youth.

"Let him ride out with the girl. Let him ride straight north. I, night and day, shall be waiting and watching for his coming. I shall have fast horses with me. It will be your part to handle the guards so that the two have a chance to get a little start. You are a strong young brave. Perhaps you will be the chief of the guards on that day."

"Perhaps," said the boy, stern and tense with excitement.

"Your own horse could stumble in the hunt. The other two or three you could first have sent back a little distance for some purpose. You could fire your rifle, and the bullet could miss the mark. These things all are possible!"

"Among the Cheyennes," said Rushing Wind, "after that day I would be counted less than a dog in worth!"

"You could leave the Cheyennes and come to us. We would make you richer than any chief."

"I would be known as a traitor. My tribe would scorn me."

"Time darkens the mind and the memory. After a little while you could come back. You would have fine horses and guns to give to the chiefs. You would have splendid knives, and horse loads of weapons and ammunition. You would make the whole tribe so happy with your return and the riches that you gave away that they would never raise a voice against you in the council."

Rushing Wind drew a great breath. His eyes were dim. The adventure was taking shape before them.

"And if you were not condemned in the council, you would be able to meet the warriors who spoke to you with anger or with scorn."

The breast of the youngster heaved with pride and with courage.

"But if you do not do this thing, no one will do it. I have been led by the dream to find you. The medicine of White Thunder is working already. It has brought me here. It fills your own heart, now. His bird is watching above us to listen to your answer. Tell me, Rushing Wind, will you deliver your people from danger, or will you not?"

Rushing Wind leaped to his feet and threw his hands above his head.

"I shall!" said he.

"Look!" said the other. "The bird has heard! He departs to carry the news to his master."

For the waiting buzzard, which rapidly had been circling lower, now, startled as the Indian sprang up, slid away through the air, rising higher, and aiming straight south and east.

Young Rushing Wind stared after it with open mouth of wonder.

"Great is the medicine of White Thunder!" said he. "I am in his hands!"

CHAPTER XX

★

Black Beaver Lies Ill

When Rushing Wind returned to the Cheyenne camp, he wrapped himself in as much dignity as he could, because his expedition had not been successful. Not that this was a matter to bring any disgrace upon him. As a matter of fact, nine-tenths of the excursions—particularly the single-handed ones—never brought any results. But they were valuable and were always encouraged by the chief. No one was more valuable during the hardships of a long march than the young man who had learned to support himself for many days, weeks, or months, riding solitary on the plains. He who had made several of these inland voyages was looked up to almost as though he had taken a scalp or counted a coup. A chief gathering a party for the warpath was sure to try to include as many of these hardy adventurers as possible.

As he crossed the river, he saw some boys swimming. They spied him at once and came for him like young greyhounds, whooping. Around him they circled, rattling questions, but when they gathered from his silence and the absence of any spoils that he had not done anything noteworthy, they left him at once, scampering back to the water. For the day was hot, the air windless. Only one careless voice called over a shoulder: "You have come back in good time, Rushing Wind. Your father is dying!"

Rushing Wind twisted about in his saddle. Then he galloped furiously for the village, quite forgetting his dignity in his fear and his grief.

He passed like a whirlwind through the village. Vaguely he

noted what lay about him. Rising Hawk had a new and larger
lodge than ever. Waiting River, in front of his tepee, was doing a
war dance all by himself, looking very like a strutting turkey cock.
In front of the home of Little Eagle seven horses were tied, and
Little Eagle was looking them over with care. Ah, Little Eagle had
a marriageable daughter, and no doubt this was the marriage price
offered by her lover!

Here, however, was his father's lodge. He flung himself from
his pony.

Smoke issued in thin breaths from the entrance; he smelled the
fragrance of the burning needles of ground pine, and knew that
some doctor must be purifying the tepee.

Softly he entered.

There were no fewer than four doctors and their women at work
in the lodge. They were walking back and forth or standing over
the sick man, shaking the rattles of buffalo skin filled with stones
to drive away the evil spirit that caused the sickness. As for Black
Beaver, he lay stiff on his bed, his face thin, cadaverous. His eyes
were half opened. They looked to Rushing Wind like the eyes of
a dead man.

Along the walls of the tent he saw his mother and the other
squaw, watching with strained eyes, already gathering in their
hearts, apparently, the fury of the death wail and the horror of the
death lament.

Rushing Wind was a bold young brave, but he trembled with
weakness and with disgust. Death seemed to him a foul, unclean
thing. Such a death as this was most horrible. But a death in the
open field, in battle—it was that for which a man was made!

He passed quickly through the weaving mass of the doctors and
their women and crouched beside the bed of his father. So dense
were the fumes of the sweet grass and the other purifying smokes
that he hardly could make out the features of the warrior. He had
to wave that smoke aside.

When his son spoke, Black Beaver merely rolled his eyes. His
skin was dry and shining. It was hot as fire to the touch. Plainly
he was out of his mind and very close indeed to death.

Rushing Wind himself felt dizzy and weak. He thought that it was the evil spirit of sickness coming out of his father's body and attacking him in turn. So he shrank back beside his mother. It was frightfully hot in the tepee. Naturally, everything was closed to keep in the purifying smoke, and the fire blazed strongly. Outside, the strong sun was pouring down its full might upon the lodge.

"How long?" he asked his mother in the sign language.

"For three weeks," said she in the same method of communication.

"What has been done for him?"

"Everything that the wise men could do! Look now! You would not think that an evil spirit could stay in the body of a warrior when so much purifying smoke is in the air!"

"No! It is wonderful!" sighed the boy. "It must be a spirit of terrible strength! What was done at the first?"

"All that should be done. Your father began to tremble with cold one night. Then he burned with fever. He was nauseated. The next day he began to take long sweat baths, and after each bath he would plunge into the river. This he did every day."

"That was good!" said the boy.

"Of course it was good! But he seemed to get worse. We called in a doctor. Still he got worse. Two doctors came. Now we have given away almost everything. There are only two horses left of the entire herd!"

In spite of himself, Rushing Wind groaned. However, he was no miser. He said at once: "Why have you not called for White Thunder?"

"I would have called him. But your father and his other wife, here, would not have him. Your father does not like his white skin and his strange ways."

"Mother," said the boy, "I will go for him now. Black Beaver is wandering in his mind. He would not know what was happening to him!"

"It is no use," said the squaw. "We have nothing to pay to White Thunder."

"But he often works for nothing."

"Your father is not a beggar, Rushing Wind!" she answered.

"He will come for my sake. You will see that he will come gladly. He is my friend."

"There is no use," repeated the squaw sadly. "I have seen men die before. Your father is rushing toward the spirits. He will leave us soon. Nothing can keep him back, now!"

Rushing Wind, however, started up and left the tent. When he stood outside the flap of the entrance and had carefully closed it behind him, he was so dizzy that he had to pause a moment before the clearer air made his head easier. It was marvelous, he thought, that such clouds of purification should not have cured his father.

He went at a run across the camp and came quickly to the lodge of White Thunder, noticeable from afar for its loftiness and for the snowy sheen of the skins of which it was composed. But when he stood close to the entrance, he heard voices and paused. He had seen a great deal of White Thunder and the great medicine man always had been simple and kind to him. However, one never could tell! These men of mystery were apt to be changeable. Suppose that when he asked the help of the great doctor the latter demanded a price and then learned that only two horses remained to the sick man!

With shame and pride, Rushing Wind flushed crimson. He knew not what to do, so he hesitated.

"Here," the complaining voice of Young Willow was saying, "the red beads should go, in a line that turns here."

"I shall do it over again," said the voice of Nancy Brett.

The brave listened with some wonder. The white girl had learned to speak good Cheyenne with marvelous speed. But, for that matter, of course the medicine of White Thunder would account for much greater marvels than this!

"Let the moccasins be," said White Thunder, yawning.

There was a cry of anger from Young Willow.

"Do you want to teach your squaw to be lazy?" she asked.

"She is not my squaw," said White Thunder.

"Ha!" said Young Willow. "The stubborn man will not see the truth! It pleases him to be wrong because he prefers to be different. Is she not living in your lodge? Does she not eat your food? Does she not wear the clothes which you give her?"

"She is not my squaw," persisted White Thunder carelessly. "She is a stolen woman. Who asked her father for her? Who paid horses to her father?"

"What horses is she worth?" asked the squaw roughly.

"Hush," said White Thunder. "You are rude, Young Willow."

"I am not rude," said the old woman. "I love her, too. But she is a baby. I speak with only one tongue. I cannot lie. How many horses is she worth? She cannot do beadwork except slowly and stupidly. She cannot flesh a hide; her wrists begin to ache. She cannot tan deerskins. She does not know how to make a lodge or even how to put it up. She cannot make arrows."

"She is a wonderful cook," said White Thunder.

There was a peal of cheerful laughter. It fell on the ear of Rushing Wind like the music of small bells. He knew that it was the white girl laughing, and he wondered at her good nature.

"Bah!" said Young Willow. "What is a bow good for when it has only one string. Besides, marriage is more than a giving of horses! It is love, and you both love one another."

"Are you sure?" asked White Thunder.

"Of course I am sure," said the squaw. "You look at each other like two calves that have only one cow for a mother. I understand about such things. I am old, but I am a woman, too!"

She cackled as she said it.

"You are old," said a heavy voice—and Rushing Wind recognized the accents of Standing Bull, that battle leader—"you are old, and you are a fool. Old age is often a troublesome guest!"

"If I am troublesome," grumbled Young Willow, "I shall go back to the lodge of my husband. I never have any thanks for the work which I do here."

"Do what you are bidden," rumbled Standing Bull. "Keep peace. Speak when you are bidden to speak. A woman's tongue grows too loose when she is old."

There was a cry of anger from Young Willow.

"Why are you here to teach me?" she demanded of Standing Bull. "Go back to your own lodge. You have wives and you have children. Why do you always sit here? Why do you come here and look at this white girl like a horse looking at the edge of the sky?"

"I shall go!" said Standing Bull, with a grunt of anger.

"Stay where you are," said White Thunder. "When Young Willow is angry, her talk is like the throwing of knives. Don't pay any attention to it. We never do!"

"I am going to get some wood," said Young Willow. "But to-day I have said something that a wise man would remember!"

She came hurrying from the lodge, and behind her was the laughter of White Thunder. Rushing Wind prepared to enter.

CHAPTER XXI

★

The Under-water Spirits

He found on entering that White Thunder and the girl were still chuckling over the departure of Young Willow in a rage, while Standing Bull sat impassive in the place of honor in the lodge, propped luxuriously against a back rest, his gaze fixed upon vacancy.

It came to the mind of Rushing Wind that there might be much in the warning which had just been given to White Thunder by the squaw; but both the girl and the white man seemed oblivious of any such thought. Rushing Wind greeted all within the house with ceremony. He was given a place. Nancy Brett, smiling as a hostess should, offered him meat from the great pot in the center of the tepee, and he ate of it, as in duty bound. Then a pipe was passed to him and he accepted it, after White Thunder had lighted it. Standing Bull inquired after the fortune of the young brave in the prairie, and the latter said simply: "I saw many days of riding, and many days of prairie and many days of blue sky. But I found nothing but buffalo."

"Long journeys make good warriors," said Standing Bull sententiously. "I, before long, if the medicine is good, will start against the Crows. I shall remember you, Rushing Wind!"

The young brave heard with eyes that sparkled. He was working his way up through the crowd of the younger warriors. Such a patron as White Thunder—and now the kindness of Standing Bull promised him a future to which the doors stood wide.

"Now," said White Thunder, "you are very welcome to us,

Rushing Wind. But is there any special reason why you have come to me?"

"My father is sick," said the young Cheyenne sadly. "It must be a very strong spirit which is harming him, because now there are ten rattles being shaken in his lodge, and still he grows sicker and sicker."

White Thunder rose at once.

"Come," said he. "I shall go with you. I heard that your father would not have me near him. Otherwise, I should have offered to help long before."

"His mind is gone now," said the son, "and his eyes are in the other world. He cannot help but let you treat him!"

They came to the lodge and at the entrance flap the steam and heat and smoke from the interior boiled out into the face of Torridon. Inside, there was a wild tangle of figures, dancing in a crazy maze, raising a dust which thickened the haze, and chanting a howling dirge in unison.

"Listen," said the son, in admiration. "Is it not wonderful that all this medicine cannot make my father well?"

Torridon stepped back from the lodge.

"Send those rascals away," he said, flushing with anger. "Send them scampering. Clear every one of them out of the lodge. Then I will come in."

Rushing Wind was in desperate woe at this request. He was fairly overcome with anguish at the thought that he might offend one of the great doctors now at work in the lodge.

He said eagerly to Torridon: "If one gun is good, two guns are better; if one doctor is good, two doctors are better!"

Torridon was too excited and angry to listen to this reasonable protest.

He exclaimed again: "Send them out, Rushing Wind, or I'll turn my back on your lodge. Send them out. I'll tell you this much: They're killing your father as surely as if they were firing bullets into him!"

Rushing Wind rolled his eyes wildly. But at length he hurried into the lodge and after a few moments the doctors began to issue forth, each puffing with his late efforts, each followed by a woman loaded down with rattles and animal masks, and other contraptions. They strode off, all turning baleful eyes upon Torridon as they went by. He had offended them before merely by the greatness of his superior medicine. But now he had interfered directly with their business, and they would never forget it, as he well knew.

He was in a gloomy state as he entered the lodge. Life in the Cheyenne community was dangerous enough already, but the professional hatred of these clever rascals would make it doubly so.

The women were on their feet when he came in, looking at him with doubt, awe, and fear in their eyes. He crossed at once to the sick man and saw that he was at death's door. Most mightily, then, did Torridon wish that he possessed some real knowledge of medicine. Instead, he had only common sense to fall back upon to save this dying man.

He ordered Rushing Wind and the squaws to roll up the sides of the lodge and to open the entrance flap. There was a groan in response. The air, they told him, was fairly rich and reeking with purifications and charms. All these were now to be dissipated! All these high-priced favors were to be blown away!

He was adamant. The tent was opened and fresher wind blew the foulness away. Yet it was very hot. The sun was relentless. The breeze hardly stirred. Torridon made up his mind at once.

"The under-water spirits," said he to Rushing Wind, "might help me to carry away the evil spirit that is in your father. He must be carried at once to the side of the river. Put two back rests together and then we will carry him! Let the women come after. They should bring robes, food, and plenty of skins to put up a little tent. Let this be done quickly!"

It was done quickly, with many frantic glances at the man of the lodge, as though they feared the veteran warrior would give up the ghost at any moment. Rushing Wind took the head of the litter. Torridon took the feet—and light enough was their burden! For the fever had wasted poor Black Beaver until he was a ghost of his powerful self.

They bore him from the camp and then up the river to a

considerable distance, so that the merry sounds of the boys at the swimming pool floated only dimly to their ears, like the broken songs of birds. Here Torridon chose a place high on the bank between two lofty trees. The tent was put up with speed and skill. Cut branches made the foundation on which the bed was laid, and Black Beaver was made warm and comfortable.

He had begun to roll his head from side to side and mutter. Sometimes the muttering rose to a harsh shout.

"He is dying!" said the younger squaw, and fell on her knees beside the bed.

"Peace!" said Torridon, who was reasonably sure that she was right. "The under-water spirits are now trying to take the evil out of him. That is why he shouts and turns. Because there is a battle going on in his heart!"

He next asked what had been eaten by Black Beaver, and was told that for three days the warrior had refused everything, even the tenderest bits of roasted venison!

No wonder he was failing rapidly—a three-day fast, a burning fever, and a lodge choked with foul air and smoke!

Torridon had a broth cooked for the sick man. Then the head of Black Beaver was supported, and the broth poured down his throat. In the end the brave lay back with a groan. His eyes closed. Torridon thought that death actually had come. Silence fell on the watching group. But presently all could see that the sick man's breast was rising and falling gently.

"That is good!" whispered Rushing Wind. "He sleeps! Oh, White Thunder, how mighty is your medicine! The others are nothing! All the other doctors are the rattling of dead leaves. You, alone, have power!"

Torridon sat down cross-legged under a tree and looked at the hushed squaws, at the tense face of Rushing Wind, and wondered at himself. All his amateur attempts at cures had been strangely successful. Those powerful frames of the Indians, toughened by a constant life in the open, seemed to need nothing but a quiet chance and no disturbance in order to fight off every ill that flesh is heir to. The torments of the "doctors," felt Torridon, had killed more than unassisted disease could have done.

He looked farther off at the prairie, wide as the sea and more level, no bush, no tree breaking its monotonous outline, and he wondered whether, when he returned to his own kind—if that ever was to be—he could accomplish among them work half so successful as that which he had managed among these red children. Among them he was a great man, he was a great spirit walking the earth by special permission of the Sky People. Among his white cousins he would be insignificant Paul Torridon once more!

So he wondered, half sadly and half with resignation. He could see that his affairs were now involved in so great a tangle that his own volition was not sufficient to straighten matters out. Nancy Brett was in his hands. That situation could not continue. Vaguely he hoped that a priest might be found, somewhere, who would be brought to the camp to perform a marriage ceremony. In the meantime he passed the days in constant dread of the future, and of himself.

That long silence on the bank of the river continued the rest of the day. About evening, the sleeper wakened. He remained restless from that point until midnight. Torridon managed to give him a little more broth, but after eating, Black Beaver became more restless still. His fever seemed higher. He groaned continually, and sometimes in the night, he broke out into frightful peals of laughter.

After midnight it was plain that he was weakening. The squaws, with desperate, drawn faces, sat by the bed, and their eyes wandered continually from their lord and master to the face of Torridon. He felt the burden of their trust, but he knew nothing that he could do.

Some hours after midnight, there was a convulsive movement of the sick man. Torridon ran to look at him and found that Black Beaver had twisted over and lay face downward. He did not stir. This time Torridon made sure that death was there.

He touched the back of Black Beaver. To his astonishment, it was drenched with perspiration. He leaned lower, and he could hear the deep faint breathing of the Cheyenne.

Once more the power had been granted to Torridon. One more

life was saved. He looked up reverently to the black of the trees, to the fainter blue-black of the sky beyond, dappled with great stars.

"He will live," said Torridon. And then he added, with irresistible charlatanry: "The under-water spirits have heard me calling to them. They have come and taken the evil spirit away!"

CHAPTER XXII

★

Standing Bull Speaks

When Torridon and Rushing Wind had left the lodge, Standing Bull showed no inclination to depart from it. As a matter of fact, it was rather a breach of etiquette for him to remain there after the man of the lodge had departed—particularly since the squaw, Young Willow, was gone out also. Nancy Brett was prefectly aware of this; however, she made light of the matter and began to talk cheerfully, in her broken Cheyenne, about the illness of Black Beaver.

The war chief listened to this talk without comment, fixing a grave eye upon her.

However, he finally said, as though to end the subject: "White Thunder will cure Black Beaver."

"He is very ill," said the girl.

"White Thunder," said the chief, "has power from the Sky People—over such matters as this!"

He added the last words with a certain significance.

And Nancy Brett, canting her head like a bird to one side, asked him gravely what he meant.

"Heammawihio," said the warrior, "is jealous of men on earth. He does not give double power to one man. The great warriors are not the great medicine men."

"White Thunder," said the girl readily, "has led the Cheyennes against the Sioux and beaten them badly. Is not that true?"

"He was with the war party," said the chief in answer. "He saw signals from the Sky People, which they had sent down because they love the Cheyennes. All that he needed to do was to read those signs. He has power to read them. Just as certain of the old men are able to read the pictures which are painted on a lodge. That is all. The eye of White Thunder is clear to read dreams. He has read my *own* dreams."

The girl suppressed a smile. She had listened to many absurd interpretations which her lover had put upon the dreams of the Indians. However, now she maintained a straight face. Apparently there was more to come, and it was not long before the chief spoke.

"But as for battle," said Standing Bull, "he never is great. He never has counted a coup. In the fight against the Dakotas, he was not in the front rank. He ran weakly behind the others."

"He killed two men, I thought," said Nancy Brett.

"The Dakotas," explained the Cheyenne, "were herded together like buffalo which do not know which way to run. A child could not have missed them with a headless arrow. But White Thunder did not count a single coup. He did not take a single scalp. When the warriors returned home, White Thunder was not seen at the war dance. He did not come to the feasts to boast."

"He never talks about what he has done," said the girl readily.

"Of course, he does not." answered Standing Bull. "And the reason is that he knows he does nothing of himself."

"Who has made rain for the Cheyennes and saved them when their corn was dying?" she asked.

"Heammawihio," answered Standing Bull, with perfect satisfaction in his face.

The girl was silent, wondering at these speeches. Standing Bull appeared in the camp as the greatest friend to Torridon. Certainly, however, he was attacking him now.

"Then," she said at last, "everything that White Thunder has seemed to do really was done by Heammawihio?"

"Everything," said the warrior. "And since he has done nothing in battle, is it not plain that Heammawihio does not wish to strike through his hand at the enemy of the Cheyennes?"

There was a certain childishness in this species of reasoning that she saw could not be answered. Therefore, she was silent.

Another thought was entering her mind. She fairly held her breath.

"In war he is weak," went on the chief. "And that is a sad thing. We have spent many days together. I have waited to see White Thunder strike down a single enemy, or count a single coup, or take a single scalp. He never will do that. His spirit turns to water. I have seen his knees shake and his face turn pale!"

His lip curled as he spoke.

"I don't think that you understand him," she ventured at last. "He always has been very high strung and nervous. He's not like other men. But I've seen him ride a wild horse that even Roger Lincoln could not ride. And I've seen him stand up to a bully three times his size. He may tremble and turn pale, but he's not afraid to attempt all sorts of things."

Standing Bull merely shook his head.

"You," said he, "are a woman, and you know nothing about battle. But I know about battle. I understand such things. You should believe what I tell you."

To this blunt speech, no rejoinder was possible.

"You, just now," went on the chief, "think that he is a very great man. You look on him kindly. You love White Thunder. Is that true?"

She answered frankly: "That is true."

"Women," said the warrior after a moment of gloomy reflection, "are like children. They see the thing that is not and they believe it to be true!"

"Perhaps," said she, rather afraid to contradict him.

"Yes, it is true. All wise men know that this is true. So you look like a child at White Thunder. You see that the children follow him, expecting marvels, and the young men talk about him, and the old men ask for his voice in the council. You would say, therefore, that the Cheyennes have no chief greater than White Thunder!"

"I would say that he is a great man among the Cheyennes," she agreed cautiously.

"But you do not know," went on Standing Bull, "that in their hearts, when they speak among themselves, all the Cheyennes despise this man!"

She was struck dumb.

"All," he went on, "except some of the young braves, like Rushing Wind. They, also, do not think clearly. Their minds are full of clouds. But the warriors who have counted many coups and taken many scalps see the truth about this white man!"

She listened, seeing that a crisis was rapidly approaching in the conversation.

"After a while," he continued, "even the younger warriors will understand White Thunder. They, also, will smile to themselves when they see him pass. And then how will you feel?"

"If I love him, I shall not care," said she.

"Why do women love men?" asked the chief.

He did not wait for an answer, but he continued swiftly: "Because a man is brave, because he does not fear the enemy, because he breaks the ranks of the Dakotas in the charge and counts coups upon them and takes their scalps!"

She could not speak. He was growing more and more excited.

"You think," he went on, "that White Thunder some day will grow older and bolder and that then he will begin to do these things, but you are wrong, for he never will do them. I, Standing Bull, will tell you that, because it is true, and I want you to know the truth!"

His breast was beginning to heave and his eyes to shine.

Then he said: "But there are others among the Cheyennes who have done these things. I, Standing Bull, have done these things. It was I who went out and dreamed by the bank of the river, with the under-water people reaching out their hands for me. It was I who went up among the Sky People and found White Thunder and brought him down to my people. All this is known to the Cheyennes. All the chiefs and even the children know of these things that I have done."

"I have heard them say so," said the girl, still careful to a degree.

"And also in their councils the old men send for me. They put me in a good place in the lodge. The medicine of Standing Bull is good, they say. It is very strong!

"When I speak, they listen. I have a strong brain. It thinks straight as a horse runs. When I speak, the Cheyennes all listen. Before long, when High Wolf dies, I shall be the greatest of the chiefs. I tell you this, because it is a thing that you ought to know."

"I have heard all the people speak well of you," she replied. "White Thunder praises you, too. He is a great friend of yours!"

She hoped that this remark might soften the humor of the chief, but it had a contrary effect.

"He cannot help but be a friend of mine," said Standing Bull. "The Sky People sent him to me. Therefore, he is forced to be my friend, but all the time, he hates me in his heart. He knows that I first brought him here. When he ran away, I went after him. I found him among the white men. They had many guns. They were great warriors. They were his friends and they were ready to strike a blow for him. But Standing Bull was not afraid. He went in among them. He took White Thunder as a mother takes a child. He carried White Thunder across the wide prairie and back to the Cheyennes, and all the people shouted and were glad to have the great medicine man among them once more. So White Thunder still pretends to be my friend but it is only because he knows that I am strong. I am stronger than he is. In spite of all his medicine, I can do what I want with him. He was given to me by the Sky People!"

In his emotion and his pride, he swayed a little from side to side, and his voice reverberated through the lodge like thunder.

The girl watched, cowering a little. She felt that there was a touch of madness in this frantic warrior.

"Also," said the chief, continuing rapidly, "I tell you that Standing Bull has counted many coups. When the coup stick is passed and they ask who has counted twelve coups, the other braves sit silent, until I am called upon, or Rising Hawk. Then I have taken six scalps. With them I am going to make a rich scalp shirt. Those scalps now are drying and curing in my lodge and they make the heart of Standing Bull great!

"Now I tell you why I am saying these things. If you stay with White Thunder, soon you will be ashamed. You will wish that you had married even the poorest of the warriors. You will wish that your man was brave and strong in battle. But I, Standing Bull, offer to take you. I will put you on a fine horse. I will carry you away. We will forget White Thunder. I have spoken!"

CHAPTER XXIII

★

Magic of White Thunder

No speech was possible to poor Nancy Brett. If an indignant denial and upbraiding burst almost to her lips, she forced it back.

This was treason of one man to his friend. But, moreover, it was something else. It was what Standing Bull considered a statement of plain fact. He wanted to spare her a dreadful humiliation and the complete ruin of her life.

He would leave his place in the nation, and for her sake strive to work out a new destiny in another tribe of the Cheyennes. Leaving his lodge, his horses, his wives, his son and daughters, he would begin a new life.

She felt the force of all these things. She felt, too, that if he were repulsed he would become an active and open enemy, not only of her but of Paul Torridon. And what an enemy he could be she was well able to guess!

So, half stunned as all these thoughts swept into her mind, she was unable to speak, but stared first at the chief, and then at the ground.

He took the burden of an immediate decision from her. He rose and said gently: "Men are like midday; clear, strong, and sudden. Women are like the evening. They are full of a soft half light. Therefore, let my words come slowly home to your mind. Then as time goes on you will see that they are true. I, Standing Bull, shall wait for you."

With this, he wrapped himself in his robe and passed out from the lodge, clothed in his pride, his self-assurance, his vast dignity.

131

She watched him going like the passing of a dreadful storm, with yet a fiercer hurricane blowing up from the horizon's verge.

She wanted to talk to Torridon at once and give him warning of what had happened. But there was no one with whom she could talk except Young Willow.

That bent crone returned to the tepee carrying wood. When she saw Nancy Brett alone, she cried out in anger, and casting down her own burden bade her run to help in carrying in the next load.

Nancy went willing enough. Any exertion which would take her mind away from her own dark troubles was welcome to her. The squaw, at the verge of the village, where the brush grew, had cut up a quantity of wood, and she stacked the arms of Nancy with a load under which she barely managed to stagger to the entrance of the lodge. Then she pitched it onto the floor and clung to a side pole, gasping for breath. Young Willow, in spite of her years, threw down a weight twice that which Nancy had been able to manage, and, scarcely breathing hard, turned to the girl with more curiosity than unkindness.

"They have let you grow up lying in bed," said Young Willow.

She took the arm of the girl in her iron-hard thumb and forefinger.

"Tush!" said the squaw. "There is nothing here. There is nothing here!"

She tossed the arm from her, but then she told Nancy to sit down and rest. On the contrary, the white girl followed her, though Young Willow scolded her all the while they went back to the brush, saying: "What! White Thunder will take your hand and find splinters in it. 'Who has made this child work?' he will say, and he will look on me with a terrible brow!"

It seemed to Nancy an ample opportunity to draw from the squaw confirmation of the viewpoint of the Indians concerning Torridon.

She said simply: "I don't think you would be very afraid of White Thunder, no matter what he said."

"You think not?" asked Young Willow shortly.

"Of course not. You are only afraid of men like your chief, High Wolf."

"Why only of him?" asked the squaw, more abrupt than ever.

"He has counted how many coups, and taken how many scalps?" asked Nancy.

"And should that make us afraid?"

"Yes. Doesn't it?"

"Of course it does. High Wolf is a famous warrior. But—he never has pulled the rain down out of the sky!"

"And White Thunder never has taken a scalp!"

The squaw stopped and peered beneath furrowed brows at the girl.

"You are like all the others," she said. "A woman is never happy until her husband beats her. I never could be sure that High Wolf was a great chief until the day when he threw a knife at me. It missed my eye by the thickness of a hair. After that I knew that I had found a master. I stopped thinking about other men. You are the same way. White Thunder is not great enough for you!"

It eased the heart of Nancy to hear this talk. Nevertheless, she wanted much more confirmation, and she went on: "White Thunder is very gentle and kind; his voice never is harsh; of course I love him. But there are other things."

"Like crushing the Dakotas? Like making the rain come down when he calls for it? Like using the birds of the sky to carry his messages and be his spies? Is that what you mean? What other men can do those things so well as White Thunder?"

"He never has taken a scalp," said Nancy, recurring to the words of Standing Bull.

"Why should he take scalps?" said the old woman fiercely. "Does he need to take scalps? When a chief has killed a buffalo, does he cut off its tail? When a chief has killed a grizzly bear, does he cut off its claws and wear them as ornaments? No, he lets the other men, the younger men, the less famous warriors, cut off the claws. He gives the claws away. That is the way with White Thunder."

"He never has joined the scalp dance. He never has joined in the war dance and boasted of what he has done!"

"The crow can caw and the blackbird can whistle," said the

squaw, "but a great man does not need to talk about himself. No more does White Thunder."

"Never once has he counted coup!"

"Listen to me, while I say the thing that is true," said the other. "He struck the Dakotas numb. He sent in the young warriors. All the fighting men rushed on the Dakotas, and the Sioux could not strike to defend themselves. With his power, White Thunder could do this. But why should he want to count coups on men who he knew were helpless? That is not his way. He knows that Heammawihio is watching everything that he does. Therefore, he does not dare to cover himself with feathers and scalps, and he does not even carry a coup stick! It is not necessary. His ways are not the ways of the other Cheyennes, and neither is his skin the same color. But you," she added with heat, "talk like a young fool. You bawl like a buffalo calf whose mother has been killed. There is no sense in what you say. You should sit at home and work very hard and thank Heammawihio for the good husband he has given to you. I, Young Willow, have known many men and seen many young warriors. I have been a wife and still am one. But I never have seen a man so great and also so kind as White Thunder!"

This speech utterly amazed Nancy. From what she had heard, she rather thought that Young Willow hated the young master for whom she drudged at the bidding of High Wolf. Certainly they constantly were jangling and wrangling, uttering proverbs aimed at one another, to the huge delight of Torridon, and the apparently constant rage of Young Willow.

But now she saw that the sourness of the old squaw was rather a habit of face than a quality of heart. She smiled to herself, and went on with Young Willow to help bear in the next load of wood.

As they drew nearer to the brush, they saw some boys, stripped for running except for the breech clout thong around the hips, getting ready for a race. When they saw the two women, they rushed headlong upon them, yelling.

"What do they mean?" cried Young Willow, alarmed. "What do they want?"

She raised a billet of wood above her head and threatened them, shouting: "You little fools! I am the squaw of High Wolf, and this is the squaw of White Thunder with me! White Thunder will wither your flesh and steal your eyesight if you displease him!"

In spite of these threats, one of the youngsters darted in, took a heavy blow on the shoulder from the cudgel, and caught both Nancy's hands.

She was cold with fear; his grip had the power of a young tiger's jaws.

He shrilled at her: "You are White Thunder's woman. Some of his medicine must be about you. Give me some little thing! I never have won a race! I am smaller than the others. Give me some little bit of medicine, and I shall carry it back to you afterward. Give something to me, and I shall win the race. They will be blinded by my dust!"

He shouted this. Other boys were pressing about her, clamoring likewise, catching at her eagerly. She almost thought that she would be torn to bits.

At her breast she had a small linen handkerchief. She took it and gave it to the first claimant, the small child who had so desperately wanted help. And off he went, whooping with delight.

The children lined up at a mark. Their race was around a tree some distance off and back to the mark again.

"What can that do for him?" said the girl to Young Willow.

Young Willow laughed. "You will see," said she. "Everything about White Thunder is full of magic. Speaking Cloud had not killed game for a whole moon. I loaned him White Thunder's bow. He killed four buffalo in one day."

Nancy might have pointed out that this handkerchief was hers and had nothing to do with White Thunder, but she said nothing. So often it was impossible to speak sense to these people.

In the meantime, the race began. They were off in a whirl, rounded the tree and came speeding back for the goal.

"Now look! Now! Do you doubt?" asked Young Willow in exultation.

Behold, the bearer of the white handkerchief was sweeping up from behind his other and larger companions. A starved-looking, wizened boy was he, half blighted in infancy by some illness. But now he came like the wind.

The boys in the lead jerked their heads over their shoulders. Their legs seemed to turn to lead. Their mouths opened. They staggered. And the youngster sped past them, half a stride the first to the line.

"White Thunder! You see what he can do?" cried Young Willow.

And even Nancy was a little staggered.

But, for that matter, she had long been convinced that her lover was the greatest of all men.

CHAPTER XXIV

★

Danger Approaches

For twenty-four hours after the crisis was passed with Black Beaver, Torridon remained close to him, teaching the awe-stricken and joyous squaws how to cook broths for the patient and gradually to increase the food as the strength returned to the sick warrior. With care, there no longer was any danger. Black Beaver was an emaciated skeleton of a man, but his eye was clear, and the joy of restored life burned in it wonderfully bright.

So Torridon, a tired man, went back to the village. On the way, he encountered a youngster bearing to him in his arms a little puppy, dead and cold. He laid the puppy at the feet of Torridon, made an offering of half a dozen beads from a grimy hand, and then stood expectant.

It had even come to that—they looked to Torridon to raise the dead to life again!

He stared at the poor dead thing with pity and sorrow.

"I shall tell you what I can do," said Torridon. "His spirit has left him and will not come back. But I shall send that spirit into the other world. There it will grow big. When you die in your turn, it will be waiting for you. It will know you and come to your feet."

The youngster stared with round eyes of grief, yet he was a little consoled, and particularly when Torridon helped him bury the puppy and said over the grave a few words of gibberish. He went bounding back to the village, and Torridon followed after, a sadder man, indeed!

He could see that his life among the Cheyennes was drawing toward a crisis. They had demanded of him one impossibility after another. By the grace of a strange fortune he had been able to meet their wishes, but that good fortune could not continue much longer, and with his first important failure, he dreaded the reaction! What would the wild warriors do?

Full of that thought he came back to the lodge and found Nancy waiting for him with an anxious eye. Young Willow was at work outside, tanning a deerskin, so that Nancy was free to tell him all that had happened.

He heard the story of Standing Bull and his treacherous proposal with an air of fixed gloom. They sat close together. And Torridon took out the slender, long, double-barreled pistol, and cleaned and loaded it with care, not conscious of what he was doing, though the girl read his mind clearly.

What could she say to him, however? What resource was left to them?

The suggestion which came was out of another mind.

Rushing Wind came that evening and took Torridon apart from the lodge. They were beyond the camp before he would speak. Then he declared all that Roger Lincoln had planned and announced that he was willing to do his share. Torridon, hearing, was half doubtful of the faith of the warrior. But like a desperate man he was of a mind to clutch at straws.

They made their plans with care. Every day, Torridon and Nancy were to make a habit of riding out from the camp with their guard around them rather late in the afternoon. Because, as Rushing Wind pointed out, in case of an actual attempt at escape succeeding, the closer the fugitives were to the night, the better for them.

The greatest difficulty, beyond that of breaking away from the guards in the first place, would be in finding a proper mount for Nancy. The best they could do was to hope that the finest animal in Torridon's herd would be swift enough for the work. This was a pinto, a strong little fellow, rather short of leg, but celebrated for iron endurance.

Through all this talk, Rushing Wind spoke nervously, uncertainly, as a man who is not at all sure that he is following the course of duty. However, as they turned back toward the camp he finally declared with some emotion: "I have given my word in exchange for my life. And the life of my father has been given to me also. May I become a coward in battle, White Thunder, and a scorn and a shame to my people, if I do not work for you in all this as if my soul were in your hands!"

With that avowal, Torridon had to rest content, though he was well aware of the shifting mind of an Indian, and the changes which a single day might produce in Rushing Wind and in his resolve.

They had no sooner got back to the camp than two eager messengers pounced on Torridon and dragged him off on an errand of the greatest haste.

They carried him to the lodge of Singing Arrow, an old and important member of the tribe. He had passed the flower of his prime as an active fighter, but he was still of great value and much respected in the council. When Torridon entered, he found Singing Arrow sitting cross-legged at the side of a young and pretty girl whom he had recently taken as a wife.

On the other side of the lodge lay a negro with close-cropped, woolly head.

And at a single glance he could tell that the negro and the girl were suffering from one ailment. Their faces were puffed. Their eyes were distended. Their breath was an alarming rattle in their throats.

The story was quickly told. The evening before, Torridon knew that a negro, apparently a runaway slave, had come to the camp riding a horse which staggered with exhaustion. The negro himself appeared weak with the long journey from the settlements. And Singing Arrow, out of the largeness of his heart, had taken him into his tepee.

Apparently, the poor black man was suffering from some highly infectious disease, and it was making terrible progress with the young squaw.

Torridon examined them in wonder. He never had seen such sickness before. The limbs seemed to be shrunken. The bodies and the faces were swollen. On the right arm of the negro, high up on the inside, there was a hard swelling beneath the skin. On the left arm of the girl there was a similar swelling. They had high fevers. Their eyes were bloodshot and rolled in delirium. Never before had Torridon seen such a thing.

He gave strong advice at once: that the negro and the squaw be moved to the edge of the camp, away from all the other lodges. That no one from this tepee should so much as speak to other members of the tribe. That the patients should be watched day and night and given only that light broth which was Torridon's staple diet for all the sick of the Cheyennes.

"The evil spirit in the body of the negro," he explained gravely, "has called on its fellows. They have passed into the body of the squaw. From her, in turn, they may pass into others."

After that he went back to his own lodge, took off the clothes he was wearing and had Young Willow hang them outside the lodge, with orders that they should not be touched again until a fortnight of wind and sun had passed over them. Then he went to sleep, very troubled. It seemed as though the great disaster which he had been fearing was already upon the Cheyennes.

In the morning, he learned that the negro and the squaw were in the same condition. The lodge had been moved, obediently, to the verge of the camp, but in doing so neighbors had given help.

Torridon shuddered when he learned this story.

However, there was another thing to occupy both Torridon and Nancy. He told her the plan that morning, and in the late afternoon, they went out together, with Ashur and the pinto. The great chief, Rising Hawk, was in person at the head of their escort on this day. With him were two young braves, scarcely past boyhood, but for that reason all the lighter on horseback, all the wilder and swifter as riders.

They passed far down the bank of the river, turned and rode in a broad circle back toward the village.

As they came nearer, a frantic horseman approached them. His news he shouted from a distance, and again in stammering haste as he came closer. Every person in the lodge of Singing Arrow was prostrate and helpless with the illness. The negro who brought the pestilence into the village was dead. And half a dozen of those

who had helped in the removal of the lodge that day were already
ill!

What was to be done? Already the medicine men of the tribe
were hard at work, purifying the lodges, treating the sufferers, but
so far they had not driven away a single devil from one sick man's
body.

Riding hastily back toward the town, they passed the sweat
house in time to see a naked man issue from it and run with
staggering steps down to the river, accompanied by a medicine
man who, with the head of a wolf above his own and a wolf's tail
flaunting at his back, bounded and pranced at the side of the sick
man.

"Stop them!" cried White Thunder. "That will kill the poor
man!"

"Who can stop a doctor when he is in the middle of a rite?"
asked Rising Hawk in sharp reproof. "If your own medicine is
stronger, go heal the rest of the sick, White Thunder!"

A harsh voice had Rising Hawk as he uttered this dictum, and
Torridon made no reply. He merely glanced at Nancy, and she
back to him.

He went back to his lodge, took off his clothes and donned the
suit which he had worn on the evening before when he entered the
lodge of Singing Arrow, and began a round of the tepees which
had sick in them. Every case was exactly the same; except for one
girl who seemed to be in great pain. The others suffered no
agony—only a numbing fever which made them unwilling to
move, even to eat.

In every case he made the same suggestion—that the whole
lodge be moved away from the camp, and a city of the sick
segregated, having no communion with the rest of the camp.

His advice was received with open anger.

"You," said one strong warrior whose son was stricken, "have
power in such matters as these. Heammawihio gave you that
power and sent you down here to take care of the Cheyennes.
Now, why don't you do something to help us? You are only giving
us words. You are not doing anything or making any medicine to
drive away the evil spirits!"

Torridon went back to his lodge sick at heart. He had the feeling that even a skillful doctor would have had his hands more than full in such a case as this, and he was sure that calamity was soon to fall upon him.

CHAPTER XXV

★

A Falling God

When he had changed from the polluted clothing and washed his body clean, he dressed, and went to the entrance of his lodge. Young Willow came to hold back the flap that he might enter.

"Don't come near me," he told her. "If you so much as touch me, you may die of it. I have been near evil spirits."

"You have washed yourself clean," said the squaw.

"It may be even in my breath," said Torridon bitterly.

"Come," said Young Willow stoutly. "I am not afraid. I have never been a man to take scalps, but I never have been afraid to do my duty. Come in. I have some fresh venison stewing in the pot. You may smell it now! Rushing Wind gave us that for a present!"

Nancy came in haste, calling softly to him, but he warned her back sharply.

He sat outside the lodge, and ate some meat from a bowl that was placed at his direction near the entrance. A robe was also passed to him. Wrapped in that, he sat back against the wall of the tepee. Nancy crouched anxiously inside.

It was the quiet of evening. The hunters all had returned. Man and boy and dog had fed and now rested. Later on, the yearning young lovers would wander out with their musical instruments and make strange noises and singing to their loved ones. But now they were quiet, and the dogs which would begin snarling and howling were now hushed also.

Dun-colored or gleaming white, like pyramids of snow, the tepees stood shadowy or bright around him. From the open entrances, soft voices spoke. Firelight wavered out upon the night through the mouths of the lodges, or in red needles darting through small punctures in the cowhides. The morrow night would not be like this, Torridon could well guess. There would be wailings and weepings for the dead!

He looked above him.

The stars were out, unblemished and clear. He felt a strange connection with them, so much had the wild tales of the Cheyennes about him entered his mind, and a sense of doom came over Torridon.

"Nancy," said he.

"Yes," she murmured. "Are you going to stay there the whole night?"

"I don't dare to breathe the same air that you may breathe after me."

"Paul, Paul," cried the girl softly, "if anything happens to you, do you think that I want to live on after you? And in such a place?"

"I've thought it out," said he. "As long as I'm here, they don't care for your comings and goings. You can do what you please. And this is what you must do. Will you listen?"

"Yes."

"Will you do what I tell you to do?"

"I'll try my best."

"Go out and take the pinto horse. He's tethered behind the lodge. Young Willow has gone to High Wolf. You're free to load the pinto with food and robes and never be suspected. Then lead him out of the village and down toward the river. Mount him and ride across. Keep on steadily to the north. Ride due north and never stop. Keep your horse jogging or walking. You'll cover more miles that way without killing your pony. When the morning comes you'll find Roger Lincoln. He's waiting there to the north for us."

"He's waiting for you, Paul. Not for us!"

"You've given your promise to do what I tell you."

"Do you think I could go?" said she.

"You must! There's no escape for the two of us. I see that now.

But there is an escape for you. Find Roger Lincoln, and tell him to go back to the fort. Once you're away—I'll find some means of escaping—after the sickness is ended and gone."

"But you'll never escape," sobbed Nancy. "You'll be visiting the lodges of the sick and you'll be sure to catch it. Then who will take care of you?"

"Such things are chance," said Torridon calmly. "A man has to face some dangers. This isn't a great one. I don't touch these poor invalids. I don't come near their breath—"

"Ah, but I know their lodges will be reeking! Six sick people, perhaps, in one tepee!"

"Nancy, we're talking about you. Will you go?"

She answered him with an equal calm: "Do you think that I love you as other women love? I mean, women who can live apart from their husbands? I'm not that way. I'd never leave you unless I were dragged away."

After that, he was silent for a time, trying to find some argument to persuade her.

"You can do nothing for me here," he said. "And you have a father and a mother to return to."

She answered bitterly: "I have no father and no mother. They drove me away from you. Following me, you came to the Cheyennes. Except for my father and mother, we would not be here now, Paul. We would be happy in a home of our own!"

"If they did wrong," said Torridon, looking as he spoke into the very heart of things, "they did it for your sake. You must not blame them too much. Besides, our lives have some meaning. Is it right to throw them away?"

Nancy strove to answer; the words were lost and stifled in faint sobs, and Torridon knew that it was useless to talk to her any longer on this subject. She would not leave him. And for the first time in his young life true humility flowed into the heart of the boy, and he wondered at her goodness, and the pure, strong soul of Nancy. He wondered if it had not been planned that all this should happen so that he should find the truth about life and about himself.

A haze drew gradually over the eyes of Torridon. The stars floated in a dim mist of thin, golden sparks. He slept.

When he wakened, the cold dew was in his hair and on his face. And from the distance, at the verge of the Cheyenne camp, he heard strange, high-pitched cries. For a moment they were a blended part and portion of his dream; then, wakening fully, he knew them for what they were—the dirges of lament.

And he could see with the mind's eye the poor squaws disfiguring themselves for warrior husbands, or a helpless child, now dead and still.

He prepared himself for the grimmest and saddest day of his life, but all his mental preparations were less than the reality.

Like a dreadful fire the pestilence was sweeping through the Cheyenne camp. In the morning, a warrior and two children lay dead, and thirty more were sick. But by noon the sick numbered more than fifty, and they were scattered through all parts of the camp.

The medicine men frantically rushing here and there were working in a frenzy to cast out the wicked spirits. But they themselves soon paid for their rashness. Four of them were stretched helpless by noon in the heat of the day, two of them howling with appeals to the spirits and with pain.

And Torridon went everywhere, grimly, from lodge to lodge. Men and women looked at him with stony eyes, heard his advice with glares, and in silence let him retire. And it began to appear to Torridon that this calamity was blamed upon him as a thing done to the whole nation out of personal malice.

He could have smiled at such childishness, but behind the sullen silence of those red men there was all the danger of drawn knives and leveled rifles. Before noon came, he knew that death was not far from him, if he had to remain in the camp.

He waited until the sun was sloping into the far west, its heat half gone. Then he mounted Ashur, and Nancy Brett joined him on the pinto.

For that was the day of days, so far as they were concerned. Rushing Wind was in command of the guard upon Torridon. And with him were two young braves.

In silence they rode out of the camp toward the river, but as they did so, young Rushing Wind was saying to the white man bitterly: "Why is it, White Thunder? What have the Cheyennes done to you? Why don't you drive away the bad spirits?"

"Rushing Wind," said Torridon, "I haven't the power to do this thing!"

"Ah, my friend," said the young brave. "I saw my father lying dead. You brought him back to life."

"He was not dead. He was only very sick."

"His eyes were half opened. His breath did not come," said Rushing Wind. "To you that may not be death, but to us, it seems death. But in a short time, you made my father strong. Already he sits up against a buffalo robe and asks for meat! But you, White Thunder, are angry with my people. You wish to punish them. Well, I am your friend and I tell you this as a friend. The Cheyennes are growing desperate. Some warrior who sees his son dying, some squaw who sees her strong husband falling sick, may run at you with a knife!"

Torridon made no reply.

For just then, out of the village, rode Rising Hawk, and with him were two tried and proved warriors, and they came straight toward Torridon and Rushing Wind.

Had some whisper of the plot to escape come to the ears of this stern young chieftain?

However, when he joined them he gave Torridon a quiet greeting, and simply fell in with the rest of the escort.

"What does it mean?" murmured Torridon to Rushing Wind.

The latter leaned far over and pretended to fumble at his girths. At the same time he whispered: "Give up any thought of escaping to-day! Rising Hawk suspects something, and he has come here to watch."

Torridon straightened in the saddle and drew a great breath. He had no doubt that Rushing Wind spoke the truth, but he also felt a vast assurance that unless he managed to escape on this day, he never would live to leave the Cheyennes on the morrow. Even as they rode down toward the river, the wailing from the camp followed them from afar, like the screaming of birds of prey in the distance.

CHAPTER XXVI

★

A Flying Start

Rising Hawk was not the only addition to the guard. Presently Standing Bull was seen coming out from the village, armed to the teeth and riding on a dun-colored pony, celebrated as the fastest of his string.

Unquestionably it looked as though the Cheyennes had heard some whisper of the proposed plan to escape. Nancy Brett swung her pony a little closer to Torridon.

"You look like death!" she said. "You must smile—talk—do something to keep them busy and get their eyes off you. Start a game!"

"What game could I start?" asked Torridon heavily, for hope had left him.

"Horse racing, then?"

"Against Ashur? They know that they wouldn't have a chance."

"Give them a flying start. Paul, Paul, this is our last chance! Do something!"

Her energy and courage shamed him into making some sort of attempt.

He said cheerfully to Rising Hawk, as that dignitary came up: "Here are the fastest ponies among all the Cheyennes. Which is the finest of them all, Rising Hawk?"

The latter swept his glance over the number.

"Who can tell which horse will win or which one will fail?" said the chief.

"Ah, well," answered Torridon, "Standing Bull would have

made a longer answer than that. He knows that his dun horse is the best one in the tribe."

Rising Hawk turned, and the long eagle feathers stirred behind his head.

"It is wrong," he declared sententiously, "to count a coup before the enemy has been touched. And no scalp is taken until it hangs at the saddle bow. There is the horse of White Thunder himself. Does he compare his pony with yours?"

"My horse," said Torridon, as though carelessly, "came from the sky, as every one knows. Standing Bull was comparing his horse with the others that were raised on the prairie. For my part, I think that your own pony, Rising Hawk, would throw dust in the eyes of the others. I have a good hatchet, here, that I would be willing to bet, if you were to run as far as to those trees and back."

It was, in fact, an excellent hatchet of the best steel, and the handle had been roughened and ornamented by the sinking of many glass beads into the wood. When Torridon picked out the hatchet from the sling that held it, Rising Hawk watched with glittering eyes.

"Hai! Standing Bull!" he called.

All the warriors drew near.

"White Thunder thinks that my pony is the fastest of all these. He offers to bet his hatchet."

Standing Bull expelled a breath with a sort of groan.

"You have a good horse," said he, "and the horse has a good rider. But I would ride for the sake of that same hatchet."

There was not a warrior in the band but had the same thought.

A course was suggested to the tree half a mile away and back. Suddenly there was dismounting and looking to girths. But Rising Hawk said sullenly: "The rest of you ride. I shall stay here with my friend, White Thunder!"

The first hope of Torridon disappeared like a thin mist. Rising Hawk did not intend that the prisoner should escape so easily! He would make surety doubly sure.

However, Torridon added in haste: "I'll ride in the same race with you. Why not? I shall start fifty steps to the rear of the others. Perhaps I can catch you."

"Perhaps," said Rising Hawk with a satisfied smile.

And, in an instant, they had lined up their horses.

Nancy Brett was to have her part, which consisted in holding her own pony to the side of the others and dropping her raised arm as a signal. Torridon reined back black Ashur to the rear. He gave Nancy one fixed look as he did so, and she nodded ever so slightly in return.

They understood one another. The heart of Torridon turned to ice, and all his nerves quivered like wires under a breaking strain. In the meantime, the Cheyennes had gathered at the mark. Every moment, Torridon expected Rising Hawk to call him closer. But though that chief twice turned in his saddle and marked the distance to which Torridon had withdrawn with the black horse, still he made no objection.

The attention of every Indian was now occupied with his pony. Those keen little animals, as though they knew what was wanted of them, began to rear and pitch and kick, and when they lined up, first one and then another strove to dart away.

Several heart-breaking minutes passed in this fashion. But at last the hand of Nancy fell, and the Cheyennes were off the mark with a loud grunting of the ponies as they struggled to get at once into full stride.

Nancy followed them one instant with her eyes. Then Ashur bore down on her.

As keen as any of the Indian horses for the race, the great black stallion had started with a lurch that almost tore Torridon from the saddle, but in an instant he had mastered the big horse with a touch on the reins and a word. He swerved to the left, and, turning her agile little pony around, Nancy fell in at the side of Ashur.

They made straight for the river, above the rocks, where the bed fanned out very broad, and a horse could be ridden easily and quickly through the shallows

At the top of the bank, they looked back and saw that the furious riders were still rushing ahead for the tree which was the turning point of their race. Rising Hawk, true to his promise, was beginning to forge into the lead.

When they turned that tree, they would see that Torridon was

not with them—was not in sight. And they would come like
demons to catch him again.

This was the heart-breaking moment of the escape for the two.
They gave each other one pale-faced glance, and then their horses
dipped down the bank. They struck the water with a splashing of
spray. Still, the blinding mist dashed up against their faces as the
animals struggled through the shallow current.

At last, firm ground was underhoof. They could see again, and
above them, dancing on the top of the bank, they saw an Indian
boy of thirteen years or more, with a bow in his hand—dancing
from side to side, his arms outspread to stop them, and his voice
raised to an anxious scream as he called for help.

Help was coming up to him rapidly, moreover. The boys from
the swimming pool, dashing ashore and catching up bows, stones,
little javelins, went leaping up the bank and then racing for the
danger point.

Torridon knew those youngsters well enough and dreaded them.
They had no war bows, to be sure, but they were accurate to a
wonderful degree with their play weapons. And a well-placed
shaft might kill! Those stones and javelins, too, would make a
formidable shower!

But now Ashur and the pinto were struggling up the bank.

They gained the ridge. Torridon pointed his double-barreled
pistol at the young Cheyenne, and he turned and bolted with a yell
of terror, dodging from side to side to avoid the expected bullet.

Backward glanced Torridon, and he saw the seven racers
coming in a wide-flung line, and their shouting went before them,
cutting the air with a sound more dreadful than the whistling of
whips.

Those shouts had sent the alarm into the village. Other men and
boys were darting out from the tepees. Still others were seen
rushing to catch horses.

And the heart of Torridon sank in him. For Ashur he had no
fear. But how could Nancy on her pinto outride these savage
horsemen?

The cloud of youths came like a torrent at them. An arrow
hissed past Torridon as he gave Ashur his head, and away they

went across the plain, north, due north, where Roger Lincoln, in the dim distance, must be waiting for them according to his promise.

Heaven bring him close—Roger Lincoln and the magic of his long rifle!

The air was filled with the glancing points of javelins. Stones leaped still farther forward into the valley. Arrows arched bravely after them. But neither the pinto nor Ashur was so much as touched. Their speed was great, and the boys were overanxious and at too long a distance.

But that was a small consolation.

At the very first bound, the black stallion had drawn away from the little pinto and had to be pulled back. Running infinitely within his mighty strength, still he was able to keep the pony extended to the uttermost. He seemed to be floating along, and the little pinto was working with all its might!

Nancy, with the same anxious thought in her mind, looked up at Torridon with dread. But she made herself smile, and at that, the heart of Torridon swelled almost to bursting with pride in her courage, with love for her beauty, with pity for the terrible fate which he saw so close before them.

There would be no mercy for him on this second time when he tried to escape. They had spared him before, but now they had watched their best braves sickening, and they had attributed their fall to Torridon's own malice. They would have his scalp and return with Ashur to the village.

As for Nancy?

He dared not think of that!

A wild wave of noise broke over the nearer bank of the river. It seemed impossible that the Cheyennes should have crossed the water so quickly, but there they came, every one of the seven racers, still riding abreast in a line that flashed like polished metal in the sun.

Torridon looked back at them almost with exultation in their skill which was redoubling the speed of their horses. He had been among these people so long that, in spite of himself, some pride in their prowess could not be kept out of his mind.

He looked again at Nancy Brett. On her more than on her horse depended the result of the race, and the first real hope came to Torridon when he saw that her pallor was decreasing, and the color beginning to flare up in her cheeks.

CHAPTER XXVII

★

Two Riderless Ponies

After all, it is not altogether strength which rides a horse, but balance, spirit, rhythm; or otherwise the greatest jockeys would be those of the strongest hands! So Nancy Brett rode well, her heart in her work, her body light in the saddle, and the stout little Indian pony flying over the ground.

They held the rushing Cheyennes behind them. Aye, and then they began to draw away, slowly and surely! So that Torridon, looking to the west and seeing the sun declining with rapidity, laughed aloud in his joy. A trembling laughter, however, so close was his terror on the heels of his exultation!

"We're winning, Nan!" he called to her. "They're falling back! They're falling back!"

She gave him a flashing smile, then returned seriously to her work, putting all her care into it—just a sufficient pull to keep up the pony's head and make it run straight, and always with her eyes before her, if perchance dangerous holes should open in the ground, or to swerve from obvious soft spots.

He, watching her, gloried in her courage and in her spirit. And never had he loved her as he loved her then, when her good riding seemed about to win.

But when he looked back again, he saw that they no longer drew away; the Cheyennes stuck stubbornly at one distance behind them.

Then he remembered with a sinking heart what had been told him more than once before—that good riding on an Indian pony in time of need consists in torturing from the suffering little hardy creatures the last ounce of force. There was an old saying, also, that a horse which a white man had abandoned as useless from exhaustion would still carry a Mexican two days, and when the Mexican gave it up, an Indian could wring another week's travel out of its pitiful bones and stumbling feet.

So Torridon kept careful watch behind, never communicating his fear to the girl.

He saw the sweat beginning to run fast from the flanks of the little horse. Then the shoulders were varnished with foam, and foam also flew back from its mouth. If only he could have transferred by magic some of the supreme quality of Ashur to this short-legged running mate!

For the lordly Ashur still floated serenely forward, careless, at ease, turning his proud head from side to side, seeming to mock the leagues before him, and the foolish pursuers.

The sun, too, seemed to stick at one place in the west, refusing to descend lower, so that Torridon could believe the miracle in the Bible. To the slaughtered host, it must surely have seemed that the night would never come, as it seemed now to anxious Torridon.

When he looked back again, he told himself that the distance between them and the Indians was as great as ever, but he knew in his heart that it was not. The pursuers were gaining, little by little.

But it was no time to alarm the girl. She was riding well, closely, with all her attention and skill. Let the Cheyennes press still closer before she began to use the whip!

She would not waste attention, or run the risk of throwing her pony out of its stride by turning to look behind; but from time to time she flashed a glance at Torridon, as though reading the progress of the race in his face.

He knew he was growing pale. He tried to smile at her; and he knew that the smile was a ghastly mockery, because she blanched, and leaned lower over the saddle bows, trying to transfer her weight forward a little and so ease the running muscles of the horse.

At last, glancing back, the leaders of the Cheyennes seemed

literally devouring the space left between them and the fugitives.
And now into the lead two were racing.

They were well-mounted boys, scarcely established as warriors, but already known for their skill and their daring on the
warpath. Light in the saddle, keen as hawks for their cruel work
to-day, they were at their best, and they forged steadily into the
lead until, at last, one of them yelled loudly in triumph, and the
other, as though spurred on by the shouter, snatched out a heavy
pistol and discharged it.

Torridon could not hear the sound of the ball. He felt that they
were still too far off to be damaged by such a fire, but he glanced
eagerly at Nancy. She gave him that quick, bright smile which
meant that all was well.

"The whip, Nan!" he cried to her.

"It's no good," she answered. "He's doing his best."

"The whip! The whip!" he begged.

She obeyed, cutting the little fellow resolutely down the flank,
and the result showed that Torridon was right. The little horse,
tossing his head, certainly added to his pace.

More and more that hawklike pair fell to the rear. And ease
began to come again over poor Torridon.

Still he was by no means sure. Struck by the whip from time to
time, the pony certainly was giving his best now. He was strung
out straight as a string from head to tail. Foam and sweat ran from
him, and his nostrils strained wide, showing the fiery-red lining as
he strove to take down deeper breaths of the vital air.

And well and truly was he running, for he was standing off the
prolonged challenge of the fastest mounts in that section of the
Cheyennes.

Slowly, slowly, the sun began to sink. It entered the region of
the horizon mist, which stood well up above the level of the plain,
and as it turned from fire to gold, Torridon smiled faintly and
looked again to Nancy. She was looking a bit white and drawn,
now, but she never flinched, and well it was that her nerve
remained steady and true.

For again the Indians were coming. The main body was some
distance back, but the two young falcons in the lead were rushing

forward with a wonderful velocity. Torridon could see that with hand and heel they were tormenting the poor horses into greater efforts. There simply was not strength in the arms of Nancy to equal those torments, and if there had been, she had not the heart for such riding.

So Torridon spoke no more to urge her. He did not need to speak, for every glance she cast at him showed her the agony in his eyes, and that was more than shouted words to her.

Far ahead he saw the streak of shadow that showed where trees were rising above the level of the plain. There, he felt, might be shelter, but he knew in his heart that there was no shelter whatever. It could be no more than the fringing of trees along the bank of a small stream that cut through the plains, and in such a meager wood there would not be a moment's hiding from the sharp eyes of the Indians.

Even that shelter it seemed impossible they should make, for the Cheyennes were pressing closer and closer.

"Nan, Nan," he cried, "for Heaven's sake make one grand effort!"

The brave flashing smile she gave him once more and began to jockey the pony as though she were sprinting him over a short course.

He looked back and studied the situation again.

They were neither losing nor gaining, now. Her utmost effort was just able to maintain the pace of the pursuers. Looking back, Torridon could see what had happened to the rest of the Cheyennes.

Well behind the two young leaders was a group of some half a dozen braves, among them Standing Bull and Rising Hawk, and, counted among the rest, the finest horsemen among the Cheyennes. But the bulk of the leaders were off on the horizon's verge.

So much the pinto had done, at least. He had sunk the majority of the Cheyenne riders. Only the chosen few remained. But Torridon groaned as he gazed back at them.

Two young devils worked in the lead. Behind them came the cream of the entire nation.

The screen of trees before him was all to which he could look forward. After that, death, perhaps! He would not let his mind go past the rising shadow.

Night, at least, would not come down in time. The sun's lower rim was barely touching the horizon, and afterward would be the long twilight—and now every moment was more than hours, sapping the strength that remained to the pinto. Gallantly, gallantly, he ran, but he had not on his back a torturing fiend to make of him a super-horse!

Now, glancing forward again, Torridon saw the screen of green rising straight before him. Beyond it was the gleam of water. Was it a fordable place? He hoped so, because the Indians behind did not swerve off to either side.

He said to Nancy: "Ride straight forward. Take the water, but not too fast, and let him walk up the farther bank. Then use what strength is left him to ride him on across the plain."

She stared at him with great eyes.

"What do you intend to do, Paul?"

He shouted furiously: "Are you going to argue? Do as I tell you!"

Her head sank a little. He felt as though he had struck her in the face, but he cared nothing for that. He had determined on a last desperate bid for their safety—for a moment's hope in their flight, at the least.

Now he was riding through the thin screen of the willows, and, as he did so, he checked the black stallion and whirled him around; the pinto already was at the water, striking it with an almost metallic crash.

As he whirled the horse about, he saw the two young Cheyennes converge their horses a little, making for the gap between the trees through which the fugitives had ridden, and now Torridon could see the grins of unearthly joy on their faces, the wild glitter of their eyes. Already they were tasting the pleasure of the coup, the death stroke, the scalping.

As for Nancy, she would be reserved—for the tepee of Standing Bull!

He raised his pistol. Both shots must bring down a man, for

otherwise it would mean sudden death, clutched by the other young tiger.

They saw that movement. One of them raised his lance and hurled it, but his horse at that moment stumbled, and though the range was short, the long, slender weapon went past Torridon's head with a soft, wavering hum which he would never forget to his death's day.

The second had caught his rifle to the ready, and from this position he fired it, missed grossly, and then swung the heavy weapon with both hands, making ready to use it as a club to dash out the brains of the white man, and the while riding and guiding the pony with the grip of his powerful knees alone.

For a fraction of a second Torridon had held his fire. Not that there was no fear in him. He was cold with it. But as had happened before in dreadful crises of his life, that fear was not benumbing. It left his brain perfectly clear.

He gave the first barrel of the pistol to the left-hand man—the lancer, who had now jerked a war club from his saddlebow. And the long years of practice which Torridon had given to that little weapon were useful now.

He took the head for his target and saw the young warrior slung from his saddle as though struck by a vast weight. The second barrel he gave to the other rider. There was no time, now, for delicate precision in aiming. He shot the man through the body and saw the grin of exultant triumph turn to a ghastly expression of horror, agony, and dreadful determination.

With the long rifle balanced for the blow, the brave rushed his pony in. Just above the head of Torridon the danger swayed, and then glanced harmlessly to the side.

The youth struck the ground with a strange and horrible jouncing sound, like the fall of a half-filled water barrel, and rolled rapidly over and over.

Two riderless ponies turned right and fled frightened among the trees.

CHAPTER XXVIII

★

With the Sunset

It affected Torridon, at that moment, like a rush of wind against him. And indeed, the dust which the horses of the two dead men had raised was still blowing up against his face. No, not like the passage of wind, but the light of two dim spirits, suddenly launched into nothingness on this calm, clear, beautiful evening.

For the sun was just down. A pillar of golden fire streaked up the western sky, and on either side of it, broad wings of crimson, feathered with purple cloud, stretched far north and south, where the horizon was all bedimmed with soft, rich colors in a band that mounted from the dun-colored earth to the incredible green of the lower sky. And above this, still, there was the evening sky, half glorious with day, and half darkened by night.

But out of that beauty rode a level rank of warriors, each a tower of strength, each terrible, now, to avenge the blood of the dead men. Seven noble Cheyennes, the glory of their race. He knew Standing Bull and Rising Hawk of old. And the others were not a whit less formidable. One of them, tipping his long rifle to his shoulder, sent a bullet hissing past the very ear of Torridon. A snap shot—and yet accurate enough even at that distance almost to end the boy's days.

Then he swerved Ashur away; the stallion crossed the water with a crash and a bound, flung up the farther bank, and went after Nancy Brett and the pinto.

When Torridon saw the distance to which she had gained, he was amazed and delighted. He was less pleased when he observed the manner in which Ashur ran up to the pony as though it were standing still.

Nancy, as he came back, turned on him a look as of one who sees the dead returned to life; but she asked no questions. Only, when the seven wild riders topped the bank of the river behind them with a yell, she cast one look to the rear.

No doubt she marked the greater distance at which the pursuit rode. No doubt she saw that the two keen hawks of the Cheyennes were nowhere in view. But when she looked forward again, she made no comment to Torridon.

They crossed a little mound in the plain; suddenly the pinto tossed its head. So suddenly did it stop that Ashur was jerked far ahead in his stride before Torridon, his heart still, could swing the stallion around.

He saw Nancy clinging to the neck of the pony, which stood, dead lame, with one forefoot lifted from the ground. Only by grace of good riding and perfect balance had Nan been able to keep on the horse at all.

Torridon rushed the black to her and held out his arms.

"He'll carry us both!"

"It's death for both of us," answered the girl. "Let me go. They—they'll pay no attention to me—they'll ride on after you—"

He answered her: "Standing Bull's riding with them!"

Leaning from the saddle, he drew her up to him, and Ashur went off with a swinging stride.

The Cheyennes, speeding behind them, raised a long cry. It seemed to Torridon that that wolflike howl never would die upon the air. It rang, and floated, and rang again, curdling the blood Like wolves, indeed, when they make sure of the kill!

And yet the stallion ran with wonderful lightness. It seemed to Torridon, at first, that he marked no difference in the length or the rhythm of the stride. Certainly, they were walking away from the red men in the rear!

But a difference there was. Nancy, clinging behind, made a secondary load which could not keep in perfect rhythm with the man in the saddle. It was not sheer poundage, only; it was the clumsy disposition of the weight that would kill Ashur.

But he showed no sign of faltering. He ran on into the red heart of the sunset, when the clouds in the sky took the full color, and almost the evening seemed brighter than the day—blood bright it was to Torridon, and like a superstitious child he caught that thought to his soul of souls and told himself that this was the end.

Back, far back fell the Cheyennes. But then they came again. Torridon, looking back, groaned with despair. It seemed as thought magic were in them, to come and come again over those weary miles of long running.

The blood-red moment passed. The sky was old gold and pink and rose and soft purples all about. And still Ashur ran on, with his double burden, against the chosen horses of the Cheyennes.

It had told upon him, however. His ears no longer pricked. And his stride was shortened from its old smooth perfection. The flick and spring were gone from his legs, and in their place came a dreadful pounding that made Torridon bite his lips in sorrow and despair.

Yet it was better, was it not, that all three of them—man and horse and woman—should die together?

So said Torridon, in his despair.

And then came a voice at his ear, like the flutter of the wind: "Oh, Paul, Heaven forgive you if you throw yourself away for me! Your life is more than my life. If you live, my soul will watch you, dear. Paul, Paul, let me go!"

He merely clutched one of the hands that she was trying to withdraw from around him. And he drew the pistol, which he had reloaded as he rode up to her from the river. It was pitifully short in range. They could circle and kill him from a distance. But at least one bullet from it would keep Nancy from them.

The time was not long.

Now, looking over his shoulder, he saw their line extending from side to side as they rushed up on him. They had had their lesson in the killing of the two headlong young warriors, and no practiced brave would throw away a single chance of safety. They saw that their prey was in their grasp, and they were aiming at a circle in which they would net him.

The fastest horses went to either flank, surging gradually forward. The slower remained behind, and one of those was Standing Bull. Torridon felt that he could almost see that face, transformed with greedy passion.

Already the flank horses were drawing up to a level with them, and the braves in the lead, looking inward, regarded Torridon with steady glances.

Though from a distance, though in the dusk of the day, he knew them; he knew their hearts.

He turned still farther in the saddle and kissed the lips of Nancy Brett.

"Nan," he murmured, "are you ready?"

"Ready!" said she.

"I'm going to stop Ashur and make him lie down. I'll fight from behind him as well as I can. But if they rush me—the first shot—"

"Yes," said she.

And she opened her eyes more widely, and smiled at him without a trace of fear, without a trace of regret, as though to her, dying with him was more than life with any other.

So, in an agony of grief and of love, he looked into her eyes.

A rifle rang; a wild yell burst from behind them, from around them. And then Nancy was crying out in a loud, excited voice.

His own eyes were dim. He had to dash his hand against them before, looking where she pointed, he saw a riderless Indian pony, and the Cheyennes scattering this way and that!

Not fast enough, it seemed, for the gun spoke again, and Torridon saw Young Crow, veteran of many a war raid, peer of all horse thieves, slayer of three Pawnees in one terrible battle, throw up his arms and topple slowly from the saddle, and then roll in a cloud of dust.

The other five, swinging their mounts around, made off as fast as their ponies would bear them from the range of this terrible marksman.

But Torridon, through the thicker shadow that lay along the ground, had marked the flash of the rifle from the top of a rising swale of ground.

And he turned to it with an hysteria of joy swelling in him.

He tried to speak, but only weak, foolish laughter would bubble from his lips.

Nancy could say the word for him, and her voice was like a prayer of thankfulness: "Roger Lincoln! Roger Lincoln. Thank the Heaven who sent him!"

CHAPTER XXIX

★

Southward Bound

As they swept up to the swale in the golden dusk, they saw Roger Lincoln rise from the grass on his knees and beckon them down to the ground. He wasted not a word on them, but, laying one rifle beside him, he began to load a second with rapid skill, all the while staring keenly through the dim light at the Cheyennes, who had wheeled together and were apparently consulting, though well out of rifle range.

Torridon and Nancy were on the ground before the big man stood up and greeted them. Even then he had barely a word for them, and the thanks that began to pour from the lips of the girl he hushed with a wave of his hand. He went on to the stallion and stood before him, hands clasped behind his back, and brows frowning.

"Here's the weak spot," said Roger Lincoln, "and its the very spot that I thought would be strong!"

He turned with an impatient exclamation and stared at Torridon. One would have thought that he was angry with him, and Torridon said feebly: "We started with Nancy on the best pony we could get, Roger. The pinto went lame, and Ashur has been carrying us both."

"I could see that!" said Roger Lincoln tersely. "You," he added sharply to the girl, "get on Comanche! Comanche, stand up!"

Out of the grass rose the famous silver mare, and beside her a tall brown gelding, the very make of speed—lean-headed, long of neck, with shoulders that promised ample power and a deep barrel—sure token of wind and heart.

"Take the brown," said Roger Lincoln to Torridon, "and lead Ashur. We have to cool him out, and it won't do to let him stand."

"And what will you do, Roger?"

"I'll run."

Nancy was about to protest, but Torridon himself silenced her.

"Lincoln knows best," he said. "Do as he says!"

He helped her into the saddle. Roger Lincoln already was running lightly before them at a stride and pace which seemed to show that he intended a long jaunt. And he bore due north.

As Torridon sprang into the saddle on the gelding, he heard Nancy murmuring: "He's furiously angry, Paul! What have we done?"

"He's not angry, I hope," said the boy. "But he's thinking hard about how he can get us out of this trouble. There's nothing else in his mind. Don't doubt Roger Lincoln. Doubt me, sooner!"

He drew on the lead rope, and Ashur broke into a stumbling trot. He was very far spent indeed, with flagging ears and dull eyes. And as Torridon rode, he kept well turned in the saddle and talked continually to the great black.

The last of life seemed to be flickering in the glazing eyes of the stallion, but under the voice of his master that light grew brighter in pulses. The jog trot, also, seemed better for him than merely standing. But still he was very far done, and his feet struck the ground shambling and uncertainly, as though they moved by a volition of their own and without the will of the horse. And it seemed to Torridon, as he looked back at the fine head of the horse, that rather than abandon Ashur he would stay behind and fight the Cheyennes single-handed.

The Indians, in the meantime, had spread far and wide across the plain, their five figures gradually dying in the dusk of the day, while Roger Lincoln still ran before Torridon and the girl with a tireless step.

They went on for nearly an hour. The dusk thickened. The last pale glow finished in the west, and then there was darkness utter and absolute.

Roger Lincoln whirled and stopped the cavalcade.

"How is Ashur?" was his first question.

"Tired, tired, Roger! He shambles like a cow."

The scout spent a moment at the side of the stallion and then said briefly: "He's only half a step from a dead horse! Here's a blanket on the ground. Can you make him lie on that?"

The stallion obeyed. Even in the darkness, Torridon could see the knees of Ashur shake violently as his weight came heavily on them. Lincoln flung another robe over the big black.

"Do you know how to rub down a horse, Paul?"

"I know."

"Work on his shoulders and chest. I'll take care of the hindquarters. You, Nancy, take the head. Rub with a wisp of that grass. We have to keep his circulation going."

He made his own two horses lie down. He had chosen a little depression in the surface in the surface of the level prairie. That faint declination of the ground and the height of the grass that grew thickly around it gave them some shelter if the Indians should attempt to spot them against the sky line of the stars. But, at the same time, it allowed the Cheyennes to creep up unobserved in turn. In a way, they had blinded themselves and were now trusting to sheer chance to keep them out of the way of those keen hunters.

But even Nancy knew well enough what this work meant. With two horses they never could escape from those bloodhounds of the plains. With Ashur once again on his feet and capable of his matchless gallop, they had at least a fighting chance.

So all three fell to work in silence, only broken when Roger Lincoln, pausing to allow his aching arms a chance or recuperation, murmured: "When I remember how Ashur pitched me into the middle of the sky—and then tried to catch me with his teeth—"

He laughed softly. And then he added: "But that shaking up was worth while. I never would have known you, Paul, except for it!"

This was all he said by way of welcoming them. Nancy, from the first, might have been a figure of wood to him, so little attention did he pay to her, but gradually she came to understand. All the heart of that hero of the frontier was bent upon the great task before him. He had no time for amenities. But all the more strongly she began to feel that every drop of blood in his veins was given to the task he had undertaken. He would die most willingly to do the thing he had in hand.

"Hush!" whispered Roger Lincoln suddenly.

It was the ghost of a hiss, rather than a word.

They stopped working. Dimly, Torridon saw Lincoln reach for his rifle and gradually bring it into position. He himself drew his pistol. They waited endless moments with thundering hearts. Then something stirred through the grass, and against the stars, not ten yards from them, Torridon saw two riders looming, the faint night light glistening on their balanced rifles. But when he raised his pistol, a hand of iron gripped his arm. He waited. For an eternity, the two Indians sat their horses side by side. Torridon could see them turning their heads. They were so near that he could hear the swish of the rising wind through the tails of their horses. And he prayed with all his might that none of the horses might make a sound, a snort, or the least noise of tearing at the grass.

That prayer was granted. Softly as they had come, the pair of ghostly forms moved away again. And at an almost mute signal, the fugitives resumed their work on the stallion.

It seemed to Torridon's trembling touch that the flabby texture of the shoulder muscles had been changing—that the old feeling, like cables of India rubber, was beginning to return to them.

He whispered softly to Roger Lincoln: "I think Ashur could go on now."

"Are you sure?"

"Almost."

"Make sure if you can."

Torridon whispered. At the mere hiss of sound, the black stallion jerked up his head from the hands of Nancy.

"Yes!" said Torridon joyously.

They stood back, and at Torridon's murmured command, the stallion rose. The other two horses got up unbidden, and it seemed now to Paul Torridon that they had risen from the warm, secure darkness of the grass to stand among the very stars.

Surely some one of those prowling Cheyennes could not fail to
see them!

Roger Lincoln was speaking quietly: "The whole crew of
Cheyennes are spilled around us over the plain. They may stumble
on us in the dark, and if they do, nothing can keep them from
cutting our throats. I think those red men see in the dark, like cats.
But, in the meantime, they're spreading their nets for us. I propose
to head back straight south, march at a walk for a couple of hours,
and then swing toward the west for an hour, then back again
toward the north. We may be running our heads into the lion's
mouth. If you don't agree to this, we'll try something else. But I
think that by this time you'd find more of them to the north than
to the south."

It seemed almost rashly bold counsel, to Torridon, but he dared
not question the wisdom of Roger Lincoln, so often proved—and
in times all as perilous as this one. He merely murmured to Nancy:
"Have you the strength to go on?"

"For days and days!" she said. "It's no longer terrible—it's a
glorious game!"

It stunned Torridon to hear her. She, slender as a child and
hardly larger, was making of this a game, while his own nerves
were chafed to the breaking point.

But he believed her. There was the wavering note of ecstasy in
that whisper of hers. And, after all, she came of wild blood, strong
blood—the blood of the clan of Brett!

He remembered them now, like so many pictures of giants,
striding across his mind, and he told himself that if she lacked
their physical size, all the more heart was hers. So she had borne
herself among the Cheyennes at the village cheerfully, with a high
head, smiling in their faces.

And Torridon felt himself growing smaller and smaller in his
soul.

Roger Lincoln had a right to such a woman as this. But he, Paul
Torridon, what claim had he?

They led their horses. Comanche was blanketed lest her silver
coat should reach the eye of the enemy, and so they started on that
southward march.

CHAPTER XXX

★

A New Man

It was an evil time for reflections of any kind. They marched steadily to the south, Lincoln first, Nancy next, and Torridon as the rear guard, his pistol in his hand. Ashur undoubtedly was recovering from the terrible strain of his journey under the double burden. His head was beginning to be held high, and when they halted once or twice, Torridon felt the flanks and found them firm, but no longer drawn by exhaustion. It doubled the courage of Torridon to note these signs.

They marched on for the greater part of an hour, and then a sudden voice cried at them: "Who is that?"

A great, harsh voice in Cheyenne!

Rising from the ground to their right, Torridon saw several Indians, faint against the stars. He himself had no voice, but that of Roger Lincoln made a growling answer: "Standing Bull. Scatter to the west. They are not in the north."

"It is Standing Bull," said one of the Indians, in a plainly audible voice.

"How could it be?" said another. "I left Standing Bull only a little while ago, and he was on a fresh horse. Why should he be walking now?"

"Mount!" said the soft voice of Roger Lincoln.

And the three of them were instantly in the saddle. The moment Torridon was on the back of the stallion he knew that once more all was well with the great black horse.

"Standing Bull!" called one of the Cheyennes.

Roger Lincoln rode calmly on, still at a walk.

...ook! Look!" cried the Cheyenne who as yet had not spoken. ...at is the great horse of White Thunder! There is no other in the ...rld with a neck and head like that!"

He had had a flash of the outline against the stars, and the Indians charged with a yell the next instant.

Torridon had a glimpse of Nancy slipping forward on the neck of her horse. He saw the long rifle of Lincoln glimmer at his shoulder, but for his own part he had something better than a rifle to work with. Light in hand, easily aimed, he was as confident of the pistol as though he held two lives in his palm.

And a sort of wild ecstasy ran through Torridon. He never had felt it before, but it was as though Indian blood had stolen into his veins, for, swerving the big stallion to the right, he drove him straight at the charging men.

He fired—a tossing head of a horse received the bullet, and down went pony and rider—the Cheyenne with a whoop of rage and dismay. He fired again; and there was an answering half-stifled yell of pain.

There were five in the party. They split to either side before this death-dealing magician.

"White Thunder!" he heard the cry. "The Sky People are fighting at his side!"

And they scattered over the plain.

Torridon found himself galloping on, Ashur like a set of springs beneath him. Roger Lincoln was ranging on his left side, Nancy on his right. And vaguely he was aware that the great Roger Lincoln had missed his target with the rifle. A long tongue of flame had spurted from the muzzle of the gun, but of the five Cheyennes, only two had fallen.

"Northwest, northwest!" called Roger Lincoln, and swung his horse in that direction.

No doubt the Cheyennes would spread the report that the party was trying to drive south.

Lincoln pulled down from a gallop, a steady jog which would shuffle the miles behind them without exhausting the horses. Plainly he expected more trouble when the morning came, if not before.

But all through that night there was not a sound of a Cheyenr
there was not a sight of them. The gray of the dawn came. The
saw one another as black silhouettes. Then features became
visible. But first of all they regarded the horses. Ashur, wonderfully recovered, seemed as light as a feather. Comanche was in
fine fettle, too; but the gelding which Roger Lincoln rode plainly
showed the strain under which it had been traveling. There was
now the weak link in the chain!

They came to a thin rivulet. There was only a trickle of water,
but they found a fairly deep pool, and there they halted. Much
work lay before them before they gained the safety of Fort
Kendry.

They washed the legs and bellies of the horses, the men doing
the labor, while Nancy was sharply commanded by Lincoln to lie
down on a blanket which he stretched for her. Flat on her back he
made her lie, her arms stretched wide.

She smiled for a time at the gray sky. A moment later her eyes
were closed in sleep!

Torridon, worried, would have wakened her, but Lincoln
forbade it.

"If we could make Fort Kendry today," he said, "it would be
worth while. But we cannot. It's a long march. She has to rest."

"The Cheyennes will never rest on this trail," Torridon assured
him. "They'll ride on it like madmen, Roger, they've had six men
shot down, and four of them, I think, are dead or nearly dead.
Their pride will boiling!"

"They'll never stop," agreed Lincoln, "and they'll never rest as
long as they can make their horses stagger on. But we can't go on
at this rate, unless we determine to leave Nancy behind us. Help
me make a shade over her eyes. Let her sleep as long as she will!"

Over two ramrods and a stick they stretched a blanket, and in
that shadow Nancy still slept while the sun rose higher and the
world was drenched in white, hot light.

The brown gelding and the mare were lying down; Ashur was
busily cropping the grass, and the two men, withdrawing to a little
knoll from which they could sweep the plain to a distance,
admired the stallion.

"Look at him," said Roger Lincoln. "You can't see more than the shadow of his ribs. The work that would have killed two ordinary horses was simply a good little work-out for him! There never will be another like him, Torridon! Never in this world!"

And Torridon agreed!

Of other things Lincoln talked, half drowsily.

"Four men for you, Paul Torridon! Four Cheyennes, at that!"

"Luck," explained Torridon. "Both times it was a question of quick shooting at close range. That was why the pistol was useful. Might live a long life before such a chance came to me again!"

"Only luck?" smiled Roger Lincoln.

"Chiefly," said Torridon. "I don't want you to think that I pose as a hero. I'm not. I've been scared white all through this."

"When you rode down at those five yelling redskins?" asked Roger Lincoln with the same good-humored smile.

"Then," said Torridon, "well, I don't know. Something came over me."

"You yelled as though you were having a jolly time of it," chuckled Lincoln.

Torridon was silent. He could not understand himself; and how could he offer an explanation? But still there was a sort of memory in his throat, where the muscles had strained in that dreadful yell.

He almost felt, in fact, as though another spirit at that moment had entered his body and directed his movements! And there was something disquieting in the calm, curious eye of Lincoln, and the little smile which was on his lips.

"Tell me, Paul—".

"Yes—if I can."

"You can. This is a simple question, this time. Were you ever so happy as you were that instant, charging the Cheyennes?"

"Happy? Good heavens, of course I've been happier!" exclaimed Torridon.

"Don't be shocked like an old maid, my lad. Think back honestly. Even when Nancy Brett, yonder, told you one day that she'd marry you, were you as happy as when you went through those Indians and split them away before you, like water before the nose of a canoe? Be honest, now!"

Torridon, desperately striving for that honesty, suddenly too[] great breath.

"I think you're right. No—I never was happy—in the sam[] way, at least. It was a sort of madness, Roger! It really was a sor[] of wildness in the head!"

"But not enough to make your pistol miss!"

"They were very close," said Torridon, vaguely feeling that this was not praise, and worried.

"They were riding like fury at you, and you at them! Most men don't shoot straight at a time like that—particularly with an old-fashioned pistol!"

He sat up straight and pointed a finger at Torridon. Every vestige of the smile was gone from his face. "Paul," said he, "you're a grand fighting man, but you never ought to stay on the frontier!"

"I don't understand!" murmured Torridon. "But, of course, I've no particular desire to stay out here!"

"You think not. But—don't stay. Go back East and starve, if that's your luck, but don't stay on the frontier!"

"Will you tell me why?"

"Because all the men out here are armed to the teeth. And there are plenty of chances for trouble."

"I don't pretend to be a hero," said Torridon, a little stiffly, "but I don't think that I'm an absolute coward, either!"

"You're not," replied Lincoln, with the same smile, half whimsical, and half cold. "You're decidedly not a coward. You're the other thing, in fact!"

"What thing, Roger? Unless you mean a bully?"

He laughed at the mere thought.

"Not a bully," said Roger Lincoln, "a tiger, Paul. Not a bully!"

Torridon stared.

"I'm trying to believe my ears," he confessed, "but I find it a pretty hard job!"

"Why?"

"Because all my life I've been afraid of people. Terribly afraid of people! They've haunted me! I've lain awake at night, hoping that I'd never meet certain men again!"

Lincoln nodded.

"You've led the life of a man who fears danger, I suppose," he said dryly. "Think over the skeleton of it! Captured from your own people by the Bretts; raised among them and given the sharp side of the elbow all your life; made to teach their young bullies in a school, and mastering the roughest of them—I know that story—"

"I had help—I couldn't do a thing with them, with my hands."

"The brain, Paul! The brain is the tool that wins battles of all kinds! After that, you tame a wild horse that no man could handle except you—"

"Only by patiently visiting him every day, because I loved him. I never dreamed of mastering him."

"But master him you did! Do you carry him, or does he carry you? When I lay on the ground with more than half a ton of that black stallion charging at me, who stood up and braved him away?"

"Afterward I—was sick with fear," said Torridon honestly.

"The girl is sent away. You are thrown into a cellar and kept for a dog's death—"

"From which you saved me, Roger, and Heaven bless you for it."

"I never could have saved you. We fought our way out, side by side. The girl was gone to the Far West. You didn't hesitate to start cruising after her. Was that the act of a timid man?"

"I would have gone anywhere with you, Roger, of course."

"You lost me on the plains. I gave you up for dead, but just as I gave you up, you turn up at the fort. By heavens, you'd joined the wild Cheyennes, and you'd become their chief medicine man!"

"It was a strange combination of circumstances. I did nothing but a few silly tricks for them. Luck was with me tremendously."

"Luck was with Columbus, too," said Lincoln dryly.

He went on: "They want you so badly that they follow you on and kidnap you at the fort. When you're not happy among them, they steal Nancy away, too. You take them in the palm of your hand. Finally, you break away and carry the girl with you—"

"Because you helped me, Roger."

"Don't interrupt! And when they follow too closely, you tur
around and kill a pair of their best fighting men!"

"They were mere youngsters!"

"Were they? And was that nest of five scorpions that you
charged back yonder a set of youngsters, too?"

"I had the night to cover me."

"So did they! But you looked through the darkness like a cat
and shot down a pair of them!"

"I don't think either of them was very badly hurt."

"Paul," said Roger Lincoln, raising his hand gravely, "let me
tell you that when I heard that terrible yell come out of your throat,
I was frightened. So were those Cheyennes. They ran as if a fiend
was after them! And just at that moment, you *were* a fiend. You
were in your glory! And I tell you, Torridon, that having had one
hot taste of blood, you're going to turn into a man-eater, unless
you keep away from temptation—such as you'll find on this
frontier!"

Torridon shook his head with conviction.

"I hope I never have to draw a gun again," he said earnestly.

"You think you hope that. You don't know yourself. We're
always confusing the self of to-day with the self of yesterday. We
don't understand that we change. Now, you know your history
better than I do. But I believe that in the beginning Robespierre
hated the sight of blood. Even the blood of a chicken was too
much for him. But in the finish, he shed tons of it."

"Am I a Robespierre?" said Paul Torridon, with a faint smile.

"You're not," answered the frontiersman, "but you're the
hardest type of gunman and natural killer that steps the face of the
earth!"

"Good heavens, Roger, what are you saying to me?"

"The gunman who is a bully," said Roger Lincoln, "soon does
murder for its own sake, and soon he's disposed of. But the deadly
fellow is the quiet man who looks always afraid of the world—
who always *is* a bit afraid—and who loves that fear thrilling in his
backbone as a dope fiend loves cocaine: the quiet, shrinking little
fellow who never speaks without asking pardon; who, neverthe-

s, by some fatality is always near danger; who always is being
orced to draw his weapons. Torridon, if you stay on the frontier
six months longer, you'll have killed six men—not Indians,
Paul—white men as good as yourself!"

He drew a long breath, and, leaning back on the hummock, he
filled his pipe and began to smoke, while Torridon, confused and
half frightened, stared at the distance and tried to recognize
himself. He could not believe that Roger Lincoln was entirely
right, but of one thing he was suddenly sure—that his old self was
dead, and that in its place there was a man whom he did not know,
wearing the name of Paul Torridon!

There was a stir. Nancy Brett came from beneath her shelter.

"Breakfast time!" said Roger Lincoln cheerfully, and got up
from the grass.

CHAPTER XXXI

★

Was He a Hero?

Whether the Cheyennes had been thrown into confusion by the failure of the fugitives to keep due north in the first place, and their then swinging south, and so had failed to guard the thrust to the northwest, the three were not able to tell at the time. But, going carefully forward, husbanding the strength of their horses as they worked back toward the direction of Fort Kendry, certain it was that no sign of the red men appeared until that wildly happy day when they rode into the fort and there passed in the street, no other than the tall form of Standing Bull, wrapped in a gorgeously painted buffalo robe, his eyes fixed blankly before him, as though he were unable to recognize the party.

Roger Lincoln was for taking the big Indian in hand at once, but Torridon dissuaded him. He pointed out that his relations with Standing Bull had been more friendly than hostile. And, at any rate, they were safely in from their long voyage over the prairie.

They took Nancy to her uncle's house, and Torridon only hung in the background long enough to hear the shrill nasal cry of joy with which her strong-armed aunt welcomed her.

Then, with Roger Lincoln, he went toward the fort.

They were welcomed effusively. On that wild frontier strange exploits took place every day, but there was a peculiar strangeness about the adventures of Torridon and Nancy Brett. The commandant sat them down at his own table, and a crowded table it was to which Roger Lincoln was asked to give the details of the escape. He gave them with the utmost consideration of Torridon; but no matter what he said, the exploits of the boy were passed

~. And if some eye lighted with wonder and turned on Paul
~rridon, the glance turned away again at once. Men want one of
~eroic appearance to fill the hero's rôle, and Torridon looked too
young, too weak, too timid, in fact, to satisfy. Every one preferred
to cast the entire glory upon Roger Lincoln. He filled the eye. He
filled the mind, and he was known to have a long tale of glory in
his past. This was treated as a crowning feat.

And as for consideration of Paul Torridon, that unlucky youth
himself blasted all opportunity when, as the party broke up, he
was heard murmuring to his friend: "How shall I ever dare to go
to Samuel Brett's house to see Nancy, Roger?"

The remark was repeated with roars of laughter.

Hero? This? Fort Kendry told itself that it knew a man, and it
could not be deceived.

But there was more trouble in store for Torridon. Some few
lingered with the commandant after the supper party had broken
up, and Torridon, with others, had gone to bed. And in the midst
of this final chatting, there was a rap at the door, and a huge young
man in rather ragged deerskins appeared before them. He wanted
Paul Torridon, he said.

"Torridon's not here," said Roger Lincoln. "But I'm his friend.
Can I give him a message? He's gone to bed, dead tired. I don't
want to disturb him unless it's very important."

The youth in the doorway stepped a little inside and ran his bold
eyes over the company.

"It might be important, it might not," said he. "That all
depends. My name is Dick Brett. I come out here with my brother,
Joe. We come hunting for a low skunk and yellow-hearted cur by
name of Paul Torridon. We heard he was here. But if he
ain't—just somebody tell him that I'm gunna be waitin' for him in
the street in front of 'Chick' Marvin's store to-morrow morning
about nine. If he comes and finishes me off, then he can take on
Joe. But if he don't come, I'm gunna hunt him down and finish
him. I guess that's about all!"

He waited a moment.

There was an uneasy instant during which the guests half
expected Roger Lincoln to attack this slanderer of his friend, but

Roger Lincoln said not a word. And Dick Brett departed unhin dered.

"What'll be done, Roger?" asked the commandant uneasily. "It's sort of a shame for a kid like that Torridon to be put on by one of Brett's size! Any relation of that same Nancy?"

"Second cousin," said Roger Lincoln smoothly. "And what do you think will happen when Torridon gets this message?"

"He'll be heading back for the open lands," chuckled the commandant.

There was a general nodding of heads.

"And what," said Roger Lincoln, "will happen if he goes out to meet the pair of them?"

"Roger," said one of the trappers, "I like you fine, and I know that you've got brains in your head. But you made a mistake about this here one. He ain't got nothin' in him. I looked him in the eye. He dropped his look! He's pretty thin stuff for the making of a man!"

Roger Lincoln looked about him with a sigh.

"I knew it would come unless I got him away quickly," said he, "but I hoped that I'd have more time than this!"

"Before we found him out to be yellow, Roger?" asked the commandant curiously.

"Before," said Lincoln, "you found him out a man-eater. Man, man, do you think I was talking for fun, to-night? Did I tell you he shot four Cheyennes out of their saddles with a pistol during that chase? And I tell you again that he'll never be stopped by those great hulks, the Bretts! Only—how can he marry Nancy after he's shed the blood of her kindred?"

"That's sounding talk," said the commandant calmly. "But you know yourself, Roger, that the kid would never dream of comin' to the scratch, unless he knew that you'd be there to back him up!"

"Then," said Roger Lincoln, "I'll tell you what I'll do. I'll let one of the rest of you carry the word to Torridon. I'll not go near him to-night or to-morrow. And Heaven help the Brett boys, is all that I have to say!"

CHAPTER XXXII

★

Time Will Tell

When Torridon heard the news, he merely lifted his head from the pillow and stared at the commandant with such gleaming eyes that that gentleman withdrew in some haste. He went thoughtfully back to his table companions.

"Roger," he said slowly, "maybe there's something in what you were saying!"

But Torridon himself merely lay awake for a few moments, staring into the darkness; then he fell into an untroubled sleep. When he wakened, he found himself singing as he sponged with cold water and then shaved. And in the midst of that singing he paused and struck himself lightly across the forehead with the back of his hand.

It was not as it had been of old. He should be cowering sick at heart in a corner. Instead, there was wine in his blood. And he remembered with a shock what Roger Lincoln had said about the hot taste of blood, never to be forgotten!

He shook that thought away. He had slept late. At seven thirty he went out from the fort to a vacant field, surrounded with fir trees, all whitened and frosted over by a slowly falling rain mist. He fired ten shots at a small sapling. When it sagged and then toppled over with a sharp, splintering sound, he cleaned his gun thoroughly, reloaded it, and went in for his breakfast.

Breakfast was over. The cook could give him only soggy, cold slices of fried bacon and cold pone, heavy as wood. Yet, with lukewarm coffee, that was a feast to Torridon. The famine of the long ride was still in his bones. He found the cook watching him

curiously. When he came out into the big yard of the fort, ⊄
men left off their occupations and regarded him with the sa
wondering, hungry eyes, as though they could not believe wh
they saw.

He asked for Roger Lincoln. Roger was not there, it appeared.
Well, he was glad of that. Roger, at least, would not be there to
see the fight! Roger would not be there to accuse him. He felt a
suddenly pang of shame as he went into the street. Those other
men, rifle raised and rifle trained, how could they stand against
the subtle speed of a pistol at short range? Ah, well, they were
Bretts; what pity need a Torridon show them?

And a terrible joy filled the blood of Torridon. He wanted to
laugh and sing. He wanted to run. But he made himself go with a
soft, quiet step, with a composed face; what wonder that his eye
was fire, then?

He went straight to the house of Samuel Brett. That huge man
in person came to the door, and when he saw Torridon he roared
with rage, and lifted up a hand like a club. From within the house
came a sharp call of Samuel's wife, and the shrill cry of
Nancy—poor Nancy!

Torridon laid his pistol mouth on the chest of the giant.

"I'm going to kill a pair of Bretts," he said quietly, "and then
I'm coming back here to find my wife. I expect the door to be
open!"

He put the pistol away and turned slowly and walked up the
street, and as food to his heart was the memory of the pale,
astonished face of Samuel Brett.

He went in the middle of the road, picking his way carefully
among the ruts and the puddles. It still rained. Once a gust of
strong wind and rain came and unsettled his hat. He paused,
deliberately raised his hat and combed the moisture from his long
hair with his fingers, settled his locks over his shoulders, replaced
the hat, and went on.

There was no one in any house. And, when he arrived there, he
found the whole population of the town at the big store. They were
like a sea at every door, at every window, and banked across the
street—Indians, whites, half-breeds, negroes, French-Canadians,

...ild as tigers, but looking to Torridon suddenly, like a very ...tle and rather awe-stricken crowd.

And in the middle of the street stood Richard Brett, huge as a ...ree and as immovable.

"He has a heart, however," said Torridon coldly to himself, "and even with a pin one could kill him. Accuracy is all one needs!"

He walked straight on, while Richard Brett pitched the butt of his rifle into the hollow of his shoulder, aimed—and still Torridon went lightly, steadily toward him. The rifle was lowered. He was close now—pistol close! And yonder at the edge of the crowd, stern of face, was the other brother, rifle ready, too.

"You treacherous, sneaking rat and woman-stealer!" bellowed Richard Brett. "Have you come to fight like a man, or to get down in the mud and crawl?"

"I've come to kill you," said Torridon pleasantly, and drew the pistol. Light, light was the metal in his fingers. He could not miss. It was as though a silken thread drew the muzzle straight to the forehead of big Dick. He, with an exclamation, snatched the rifle butt once more to the hollow of his shoulder. How slow and blundering seemed the motion to Torridon!

There was almost time to pause and smile at it—then he fired, and Brett fell, the gun discharging as he went down, face foremost. And smiling indeed was Torridon as he went on, the pistol hanging at his side. The second brother had disappeared!

There was a whirl and eddy in the crowd where he had been standing, and then red fury took Torridon, and red drunken joy in killing. He ran like a greyhound for a hare. He rushed through the crowd—they gave back suddenly before him, split away as by a vast hand of fear. He hurried into the store. He peered under draped counters and tables. He ran out into the back yard.

Slowly, his teeth gritting, he came back to the street and looked up and down. Another day, then, for the second brother. Then he saw men carrying a prostrate form, a sagging body, toward the door of the store—Richard Brett, who lifted his head a little, despite the red wound in his forehead! That head was turning, and Torridon saw a crimson gash down the side of it. Then he

understood—the bullet had slipped off the bone, and glanc
around the scalp.

He stepped to the wounded man and touched his shoulder. Fea
made the eyes of Dick Brett bulge in his head.

"There will be another day for you and me!" said Torridon.

Then he turned back down the street, past white, icy faces, and
eyes that looked at him as though he were a column of fire. A
great voice called. And there was Roger Lincoln beside him,
walking with him toward the house of Samuel Brett.

"Paul," said the frontiersman, "before you go into the house,
ask yourself if you're a safe man to be her husband! I warned you
about yourself before. Was I right, or was I wrong?"

Torridon paused. And as he paused, darkness ran over his brain.
He found himself repeating: "What have I done, Roger?"

"Nearly killed one man; tried to kill two. And now you're going
to marry Nancy Brett to a gun fighter with not three years of
slaughter before him, perhaps!"

Torridon caught at the arm of Lincoln.

"Oh! Oh!" he groaned. "What's happened to me? I don't know
myself! Roger, what shall I do? What shall I do? Shall I turn back?
Shall I leave Nan?"

Roger Lincoln held him off at arm's length.

"You're past the help of any man," said he. "But maybe—wait
here!"

They were in front of the house of Samuel Brett, and Roger
Lincoln went into it, leaving Torridon stunned, feeble, in front of
the place. The wind was shaking the rain clouds to bits. Long rifts
and streaks of blue appeared in the sky. And the poplars around
the Brett house began to shine like silver—like silver mist was the
smoke which rose languidly from the chimney top.

It was to Torridon like a dissolution of the world; and his own
self had dissolved before it. He was a new man; what manner of
man he hardly could tell, but those words of Roger Lincoln in the
prairie came hauntingly through his mind—he saw the train of his
life behind him, the superdelicacy, the hypersensitiveness of his
body, of his very soul. And brutal chance had taken him in hand

d hammered and hardened him until, at last, he had been
hanged from flesh to metal.

Aye, at that very moment, half his heart was back up the street,
yearning to hunt down that other who had fled, savagely yearning.

Something came down slowly toward him. It was a shape of
mist to him, in his rush of thoughts. But those thoughts cleared,
and like a light through a storm he saw Nancy coming to him. And
a wild torrent of emotion made Torridon fall on his knees before
her, and take both her hands.

They trembled under his touch.

"Nan," he cried wildly, "tell me, for Heaven's sake, that you
have no fear of me!"

She drew him up to her, her slender arms about him.

"Don't you see, Paul?" she said to him. "I've always been
afraid of you from that first day in the schoolhouse. I always knew
that this day would come. I always feared you, and I always loved
you, too!"